# THE CHRONICLES OF

®

T

# THE CHRONICLES OF
# CONAN ®
## VOLUME 1

# TOWER OF THE ELEPHANT
## AND OTHER STORIES

based on the classic pulp
character Conan the Barbarian,
created by

## ROBERT E. HOWARD

written by

## ROY THOMAS

illustrated by

## BARRY WINDSOR-SMITH

and others

coloring by

## PETER DAWES, IAN SOKOLIWSKI,
## DENNIS KASHTON, and WIL GLASS
## at DIGITAL CHAMELEON

## DARK HORSE BOOKS™

publisher
## MIKE RICHARDSON

collection designer
## DARIN FABRICK

art director
## MARK COX

collection editors
## JEREMY BARLOW and SCOTT ALLIE

special thanks to Fredrik Malmberg and Theodore Bergquist at Conan Properties, Arthur Lieberman at Lieberman & Norwalk, Marco Lupoi at Panini, Dag Lonsjo at Bladkompaniet A. S., Jesus Pece at Planeta, Wil Glass at Digital Chameleon, Erik Ko at UDON Entertainment, and Lance Kreiter.

This volume collects issues one through eight of the original Marvel comic-book series from 1970-71.

Published by
Dark Horse Comics, Inc.
10956 SE Main Street
Milwaukie, OR 97222

www.darkhorse.com
www.conan.com

To find a comics shop in your area, call the Comic Shop Locator Service toll-free at 1-888-266-4226

First edition:
ISBN: 1-59307-016-0

3 5 7 9 10 8 6 4 2

Printed in Hong Kong

# TABLE OF CONTENTS

All stories written by Roy Thomas, Pencil art by Barry Windsor-Smith

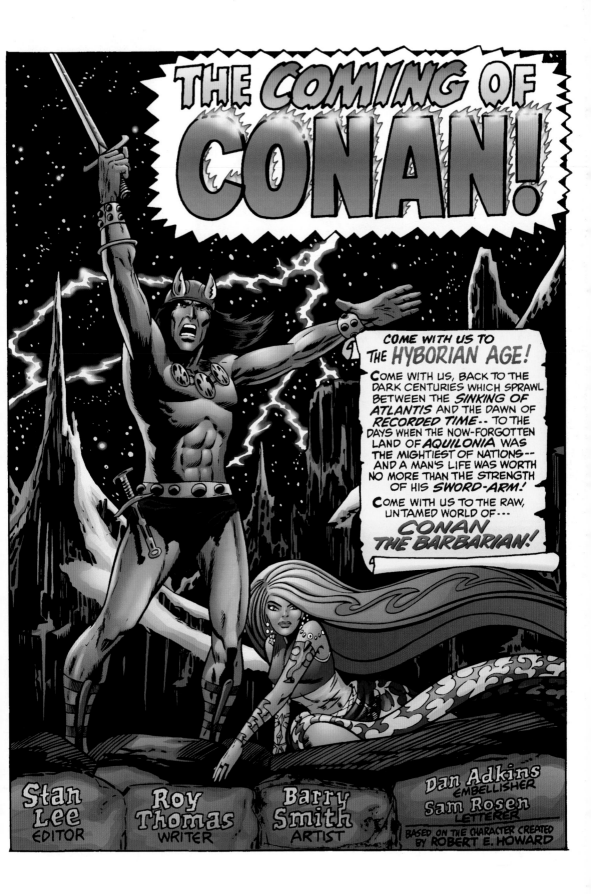

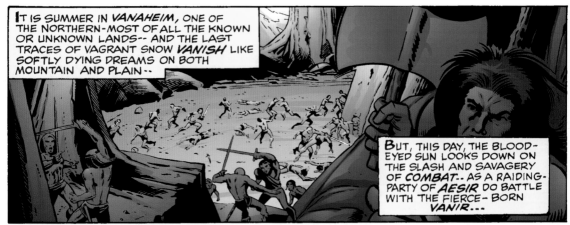

IT IS SUMMER IN *VANAHEIM*, ONE OF THE NORTHERN-MOST OF ALL THE KNOWN OR UNKNOWN LANDS-- AND THE LAST TRACES OF VAGRANT SNOW *VANISH* LIKE SOFTLY DYING DREAMS ON BOTH MOUNTAIN AND PLAIN--

BUT, THIS DAY, THE BLOOD-EYED SUN LOOKS DOWN ON THE SLASH AND SAVAGERY OF *COMBAT*-- AS A RAIDING-PARTY OF *AESIR* DO BATTLE WITH THE FIERCE-BORN *VANIR*---

AND *FOREMOST* AMONG THE SKIRMISHING, ROARING BARBARIANS IS ONE WITH LOCKS OF DARKEST *JET*--

SPEAK YOUR *PRAYERS*, STRIPLING-- FOR *CAMP-SONGS* ARE SUNG IN VANAHEIM OF THE PROWESS OF *GONDUR*.

MY LIFE IS FOR ME TO *GIVE*.. NOT FOR YOU TO *TAKE*.

AND.. I DO NOT *CHOOSE* TO GIVE IT.

YET, PERHAPS MEN *SHALL* SING ONE LAST SONG OF BOASTFUL GONDUR.

IF SO, THEY'LL SAY HE WAS THE *FIRST* MAN OF THE VANIR TO FALL BEFORE THE SLICING SWORD OF..

--CONAN THE CIMMERIAN!

8

CONAN THE CIMMERIAN! IN TIME TO COME, A NAME TO CONJURE WITH. BUT NOW, CONAN IS MERELY A MIGHTY-THEWED *YOUTH*, FRESH FROM HIS FIRST TASTE OF BATTLE AT *VENARIUM* -- AND BECOME A *MERCENARY* WITH THIS RAIDING-BAND FROM THE NEARBY BORDERS OF WIND-SWEPT *AESGAARD*---

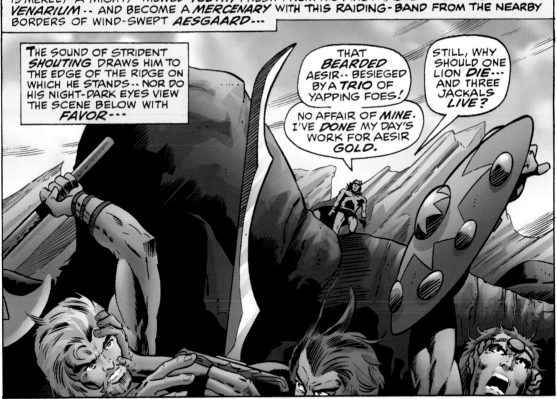

THE SOUND OF STRIDENT *SHOUTING* DRAWS HIM TO THE EDGE OF THE RIDGE ON WHICH HE STANDS-- NOR DO HIS NIGHT-DARK EYES VIEW THE SCENE BELOW WITH *FAVOR*---

THAT *BEARDED* AESIR-- BESIEGED BY A *TRIO* OF YAPPING FOES!

NO AFFAIR OF *MINE*. I'VE *DONE* MY DAY'S WORK FOR AESIR *GOLD*.

STILL, WHY SHOULD ONE LION *DIE*-- AND THREE JACKALS *LIVE*?

BY CROM! THEY *SHOULD* NOT--!

AND, *BY CROM*-- THEY *SHALL* NOT!!

9

THEN, HIS BLADE CUTTING A DEADLY ARC, THE GRIM YOUTH **WADES THRU** THE CLANGOR OF BATTLE---

... ALL THE TIME SEEING **NOTHING** SAVE THE VALIANT BEARDED AESIR AND THE THREE WHO **BESET** HIM---

HE IS **DOWN!** THE TALL ONE IS **FALLEN!**

THEN--**STRIKE**--FOR WE CANNOT **HOLD** HIM LONG--!

YOU VANIR **DOGS!** I'LL--

THE NEXT INSTANT--A BOLT OF LIVING **LIGHTNING**--AND TWO MEN OF VANAHEIM SHALL NEVER RISE **AGAIN**---

**HAH!** IF YOU CAN HANDLE **TWO** OF THESE PIGS, DARK-HAIR---

SURELY OLAV WILL HAVE NO TROUBLE WITH THE **THIRD.**

I NEVER THOUGHT YOU **WOULD,** MY FRIEND.

**INSOLENT YOUTH!** JUST BECAUSE YOU **SAVED MY LIFE,** DON'T DARE TO CALL ME **FRIEND** UNTIL I **TELL** Y--

**WAIT!** WHAT IS IT THE **OTHERS** ARE SHOUTING?

THEY'RE *FLEEING.* THEN-- *WE'VE WON!*

THAT'LL TEACH THOSE RED-HAIRED SCUM TO COME SNEAKING OVER *OUR* BORDERS -- WHEN THEY CAN'T EVEN DEFEND THEIR *OWN.*

LET'S GO *AFTER* THEM!

*DON'T* CHASE THEM! LET THEM *RUN!*

HE'S *RIGHT,* LADS. FIRST WE BIND OUR WOUNDS AND BURY OUR DEAD.

TIME ENOUGH *THEN* TO CARRY THE FIGHT TO THE DOGS' OWN CAMP.

YOU TAKE COMMAND *QUICKLY,* BOY, FOR ONE I SAW JOIN OUR PARTY ONLY *THIS MORNING...* BUT YOU DON'T SEEM TO KNOW IT'S *OLAV* WHO GIVES THE ORDERS HERE.

WHAT IS YOUR NAME?

I AM CONAN... A CIMMERIAN.

AND A *YOUNG* ONE, AT THAT. YOU'RE A LONG WAY FROM *HOME,* BOY.

GOT THE *WANDERLUST,* EH? WELL, YOU SAVED MY WEATHERED *HIDE,* SURE ENOUGH.. AND HERE'S MY *HAND* FOR IT!

TELL ME.. WHY'D YOU JOIN *OUR* BAND, INSTEAD OF *THEIRS?* WE BOTH PAY OFF IN GOOD NORTHERN GOLD.

BUT YOU AESIR PAY *MORE.*

AN *HONEST* CIMMERIAN, EH? WELL, OLAV *LIKES* THAT.

NOW, I FIGURE THAT THOSE DOGS WILL STOP TO REST IN THAT *PASS* YONDER... SO WE'LL CLIMB AROUND AND ATTACK THEM FROM *ABOVE.*

WHAT THINK YOU OF *THAT,* LAD?

YOU *PAY...* SO YOU *LEAD.*

YOU KNOW, CONAN... I THINK PERHAPS YOU ARE *TOO* HONEST.

AND BESIDES ... YOU *TALK* TOO MUCH.

WHILE, NOT FAR DISTANT, BEHIND HASTILY ERECTED DEFENSES, THE BONE-WEARY MEN OF *VANAHEIM* WEIGH THEIR CHANCES...

ANOTHER *STRAGGLER* ...BEARING HIS *DEAD* COMRADE.

*CURSED* BE THE DAY WE FIRST *LOOTED* THE BORDER TOWNS OF *AESGAARD!*

*SOFT*, LAD. LEST YOUR GRUMBLING REACH THE EARS OF *VOLFF* HIMSELF!

THIS MORNING WE *OUT-NUMBERED* OUR FOEMEN. NOW, OUR FORCES ARE *HALVED.*

AND, *APART* FROM HIS MEN SITS THEIR LEADER... TALL AND LITHE, HIS MIND ALIVE WITH THE WILD CUNNING OF THE BEAST WHOSE HIDE HE WEARS... THE WILY *VOLFF!*

THE MEN GROW *RESTIVE*, MIGHTY ONE.. *FEARFUL...*

AND NOT WITHOUT *CAUSE*, HOTHAR. WITH GONDUR *DEAD*, WE HAVE *NO WARRIOR* WHO CAN STAND AGAINST GRIM *OLAV...* OR THE DARK-HAIRED CUR WHO *SAVED* HIM.

MY MEN ARE *CUTTHROATS*, BUT NOT *STUPID* ONES.

THEY KNOW FULL WELL THAT ERE THE SUN SETS, THEY'LL HOLD THIS GORGE WITH THEIR *LIFE'S BLOOD!*

BUT, JUST BECAUSE *THEY* MUST DIE, HOTHAR...

DOES IT FOLLOW THAT *WE* MUST PERISH *WITH* THEM?

I SEE YOUR *MEANING*, GREAT VOLFF...

MEN OF THE NORTHLANDS, HEED MY WORDS. HOTHAR AND I GO TO CALL UPON THE *GODS*, TO SEEK THEIR *FAVOR* THIS DAY.

YOU WILL REMAIN *HERE*, UNTIL THE HOUR WHEN WE *RETURN.*

AY, VOLFF...

...YOU SAID OUR MEN WEREN'T *FOOLS*, GREAT VOLFF.

YET, DID *CATTLE* EVER AWAIT SLAUGHTER MORE *WILLINGLY?*

THEY'LL *FLEE*, AFTER THEY'VE *MULLED IT OVER* LONG ENOUGH.

BUT EVEN THEN, THEY'LL FORM A *BUFFER* BETWEEN US AND THE VENGEFUL *AESIR.*

*HO!* WHAT'S *THIS* I SEE BEFORE ME?

A *CAVE*... WITH STRANGE *SYMBOLS* ABOVE ITS ENTRANCE...

...AND A *GHOSTLY GLOW* FROM SOMEWHERE *WITHIN.*

*COME*... LET'S SEE WHAT LIES *BEYOND* THESE STONE PORTALS.

*ENTER*, VOLFF. *ENTER*, HOTHAR.

I HAVE BEEN ...*WAITING* FOR YOU.

AN *OLD MAN*, AS THIN AS *DEATH* ITSELF... AND A *YOUNG GIRL!*

*WHO* ARE THEY, TO DWELL IN THESE LONELY HILLS... AND HOW DID THE OLD ONE KNOW OUR *NAMES?*

*THAT* WE'LL LEARN, HOTHAR, WHEN WE *ACCEPT* THEIR INVITATION.

PERHAPS THEY CAN GUIDE US *THROUGH* THESE MOUNTAINS... TO A PLACE WHERE OUR PURSUERS CAN *NEVER* FIND US.

*FOLLOW* ME. BUT BE ON GUARD FOR *AESIR TRICKERY.*

13

YOU'LL FIND NO GOLD-TRESSED TREACHERY *HERE*, WILY ONE.

*MY* HAIR, WHEN I DID HAVE IT, WAS *SCARLET* AS YOUR OWN.

*BY THE GODS!* THIS PLACE IS A *CAVE* WITHOUT-- AND A *TEMPLE* WITHIN.

IF NAUGHT ELSE, WE CAN *HIDE* HERE FOR A TIME.

I STILL SAY... *BEWARE!*

AND *I* SAY, SCOFFER, THAT YOU NEED NOT FEAR *SHARKOSH*-- HE WHO IS CALLED *THE SHAMAN!*

YOUR COMING WAS *FORETOLD* TO ME IN A VISION I HAD, WHEN LAST I GAZED INTO YONDER *STAR-STONE.*

YEARS AGO, IT FELL FROM THE MANY-JEWELED *SKY*...

THEN, PERHAPS YOU CAN CALL UP FORCES WHICH MAY YET BRING ME *VICTORY!?*

THAT I *CAN*... FOR A *PRICE.*

I HAVE NEED OF A STRONG YOUNG *WARRIOR CAPTIVE*... FAR *MIGHTIER* THAN EITHER OF YOU.

THERE BE SUCH AMONG YOUR *FOEMEN*, NO?

*AYE.* YOUR WORDS WOULD BEST FIT A YOUTHFUL *DARK-HAIR* WHO BATTLES ON THE SIDE OF THE AESIR.

BUT TELL ME... WITH THE POWERS YOU SAY YOU HAVE, *WHY* DO YOU NEED SUCH A ONE?

THAT IS *MY* AFFAIR.

SUFFICE IT TO SAY, IT CONCERNS THE BEAUTEOUS *HANDMAIDEN* WHO SITS BESIDE ME ---

--- SHE WHOSE SMILE HAS MADE MORE *BEARABLE* AN OLD MAN'S SELF-EXILE.

WELL? ARE MY TERMS *AGREED TO?*

WHAT HAVE I TO LOSE? *UN-LEASH* YOUR PHANTOM ARMY!

I HAVE *NO NEED* OF A FULL ARMY, MAN OF THE VANIR.

NOW BE *SILENT*... AND YOU WILL OBSERVE MARVELS SUCH AS ARE *WHISPERED* ABOUT, OVER SLOWLY DYING CAMPFIRES---!

THEN, FROM THE OLD SHAMAN'S *LIPS* HISSES AN INCANTATION THAT WAS OLD WHEN *ATLANTIS* SANK... A SPELL SUCH AS ONCE WAS MUTTERED AMONG THE PURPLE-TOWERED CITIES OF ANCIENT, EVIL *ACHERON.*

A *LIVING FIRE* SEEMS TO GROW, UNBANKED, WITHIN THE SKY-SENT JEWEL... AN EERIE, PUTRID *GLOW* FILLS EACH CREVICE OF THE ROCK-HEWN CHAMBER---

--AND THEN, THE STAR-STONE BEGINS TO *HUM*...!

THE *VANIR* SKULK ABOUT BELOW, SUSPECTING *NOTHING.*

YOU WERE *WISELY* CHOSEN TO AVENGE THE RECENT BORDER RAIDS, OLAV.

BUT WHY DO YOU *SCOWL* SO?

BECAUSE, STRIPLING, THEIR LEADER *VOLFF* IS NOT AMONG THEM.

HE MUST HAVE *FLED,* HIS NOSE SNIFFING *DISASTER* IN THE WIND.

HOW CAN THE ESCAPE OF *ONE LONE FOE* MAR YOUR JOY, OLAV?

YOU DON'T *KNOW* HIM, CONAN.

AS LONG AS HE LIVES, NO AESIR CAN SLEEP WITH *BOTH EYES* CLOSED.

STILL, WE OF AESGAARD HAVE A SAYING: "*IF THE WOLF* BE NOT AT HOME WHEN YOU COME TO CALL...

"...THEN *SLAY ITS PUPS!*"

*ATTACK,* MY BROTHERS!

15

THE AESIR HAVE FOUND US!

VOLFF! WHERE IS VOLFF THE WILY?

PERHAPS YOU'LL *GREET* HIM ONE DAY SOON ... IN THE *HALL OF SHADES.*

AND NOW... *HOLD!*

WHAT *SOUND* IS THAT... LIKE THE BEATING OF A THOUSAND ANGRY *WINGS?*

NOT A *THOUSAND,* YOUTH.... ONLY *THREE PAIRS...* BUT FIXED TO THE BODIES OF *MONSTERS!*

*LOOK,* THERE IN THE *HEAVENS*-- AT THE HORRID *DEMON-HORDE* WHICH DESCENDS UPON US!

*CROM!*

*FLEE!* WHAT MAN-FORGED BLADE CAN FEND OFF BAT-WINGED *DEVILS?*

DOWN UPON THE STARTLED TRIBESMEN SWOOP THE *TRIO FROM BEYOND*... NOR DO THEY SPARE EITHER *AESIR* OR *VANIR* IN THEIR DEADLY, VOICELESS ASSAULT...

YET, *ONE MAN* STANDS HIS GROUND, AND IS REWARDED BY A CRY SUCH AS *NO LIVING MAN* HAS HEARD...

VRAAAA

THE THINGS CAN BE *HURT!*

THEN *TO ME,* LADS ---WE'LL *STILL* SAVE THE DAY!

BUT, THE DAY IS *NOT* FOR SAVING...AS A PINIONED SHAPE SPRINGS UPON OLAV FROM *BEHIND*...

...AND HE CRUMPLES IN A LIFELESS *HEAP!*

OLAV... DEAD!

FOR THE PAST FEW FATEFUL SECONDS, YOUNG CONAN HAS *HELD BACK* FROM THE ONE-SIDED BATTLE ---FOR, ABOVE ALL ELSE, THE BARBAROUS CIMMERIANS DO FEAR THINGS *SUPERNATURAL!* BUT NOW, AT THE SIGHT OF A VALIANT LIFE SNUFFED OUT LIKE THE MEREST CANDLE, THE FEAR-SPELL IS *BROKEN*...!

BE YOU *DEMON* OR *DIVINE*--HEAVEN-SENT OR SPAWNED IN *HELL*...

AND NOW, BLACK TALONS TWITCH FOR *MY* THROAT.

OLAV SHALL BE *AVENGED!!*

But the barbarian's only *ANSWER* is the forceful flapping of two dark *WINGS* ... a sudden sensation of *WEIGHTLESSNESS* which loosens his sword-grip...

...A BONY *HAND* AGAINST WHICH ALL HIS YOUTHFUL STRENGTH IS USELESS...

...THEN, THE FEELING OF BEING *DROPPED*, LIKE SOME BROKEN RAG DOLL, TOWARDS PEAKS ON WHICH A BLANKET OF SNOW STILL LINGERS...

...AND FINALLY, A NAMELESS, ALL-CONSUMING *BLACKNESS!*

18

AN ETERNITY LATER, CONAN DRIFTS *BACK* TO THE WAKING WORLD, ESCORTED BY THE TOUCH OF SOFT FINGERS--- THE WAFTING TRACE OF AN EXOTIC SCENT--- THE CARESS OF A GIRL'S HUSHED VOICE.

*ARISE,* YOUNG BARBARIAN. YOUR TIME IS ALMOST COME.

WHO *CALLS* CONAN--- BACK FROM THE PLACE OF DREAMS?

I AM *TARA,* SO-CALLED BY THE GREAT *SHAMAN.*

*SHAMAN?* AM I, THEN, THE *PRISONER OF A SORCERER?*

YOU SPEAK *QUICKLY* TO THE POINT. MY MASTER *IS* PERHAPS A SORCERER OF SORTS--- BUT HIS POWERS ARE NOT TRULY HIS *OWN.*

THEY ALL DERIVE FROM THE *STAR-STONE...* WHICH FORETOLD EVEN THAT *YOU* WOULD BE DELIVERED UNTO US.

WHAT DOES HE *WANT* OF ME? AM I TO BE *SACRIFICED* UPON SOME PAGAN ALTAR?

*NO,* HANDSOME ONE. THERE SHALL BE NO SACRIFICE... BUT ONLY A *TRADE.*

A *TRADE?* BUT WHAT--?

SAY NO MORE, BUT KEEP *SILENT.*

THROUGH YON WOODEN BARS, THE *CEREMONY* BEGINS...

THEN, CONAN'S BLOOD RUNS COLD AS HE BEHOLDS ANEW THE *WINGED DEMONS...* NEAR THEM, TWO SMIRKING *VANIR...* AND A WIZENED OLD ONE WHO CAN ONLY BE... THE *SHAMAN.*

O STAR-STONE... SACRED JEWEL WHICH FELL LIKE RAIN FROM ON HIGH---

THE VANIR-MEN BE STILL *SCOFFERS...* NOT *TRUE BELIEVERS* IN YOUR AWESOME POWER.

GIVE US A *SIGN* OF THAT POWER, SO THAT THE *CEREMONY TRANSFERAL* MAY BE ACCOMPLISHED.

THEN, BEFORE THE AMAZED EYES OF VANIR AND CIMMERIAN ALIKE, A *VISION* FILLS THE DARKENED CHAMBER-- A SCENE OF A *WORLD-THAT-ONCE-WAS*...

BEHOLD *VALUSIA*... MIGHTIEST MAINLAND KINGDOM IN THE DAYS BEFORE *ATLANTIS* SANK.

EVEN *I* HAVE NE'ER BEFORE DELVED SO FAR INTO THE *PAST.*

MORE, GREAT STONE... TELL US *MORE!*

YES, SHAMAN AND SAVAGES... GAZE *DEEPLY*... SEE THE *LATTER DAYS* OF VALUSIA, WHEN THE LAND WAS OFT RULED BY *BARBARIAN MONARCHS*...

...AND WHEN THE *GREATEST* OF THESE USURPERS WAS THE OUTCAST ATLANTEAN... *KING KULL!*

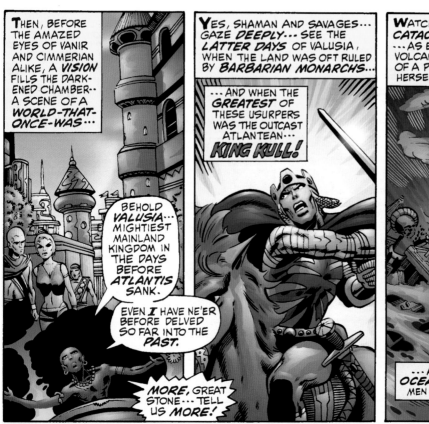

WATCH IN HORROR NOW, AS THE *CATACLYSM* ROCKS THE WORLD ...AS EARTHQUAKES AND VOLCANOES CHANGE THE FACE OF A PLANET...AS *VALUSIA* HERSELF FADES INTO LEGEND...

...AND THE THIRST-CRAZED *OCEANS* DRINK THE ISLAND MEN CALLED *ATLANTIS!*

NEXT, BEHOLD A *BABY* BORN NOT *TWENTY WINTERS AGO*... ON A BATTLEFIELD IN CIMMERIA, AMID A RAID BY THE FEARSOME *VANIR*...

LOOK UPON THAT BABE, NOW GROWN TO YOUNG *MANHOOD*... RECEIVING HIS BAPTISM OF FIRE AND SWORD AT DISTANT *VENARIUM,* BUT A WINTER GONE...

AND NOW, BE WITNESS TO THE MOST *AWESOME* SIGHT OF ALL...

...AS THIS BARBARIAN, AMIDST A HAILING POPULACE, CROWNS HIMSELF *KING* OF A MIGHTY *HYBORIAN EMPIRE!*

**HOLD!**

'TIS NOT THE *PAST* WE SEE NOW-- BUT THE *FUTURE*.

YET, THE CIMMERIAN CAN *HAVE* NO FUTURE --FOR HE IS TO BE OFFERED UP IN THE *CEREMONY OF TRANSFERRAL*.

I MUST SEE *MORE*... STILL *MORE!*

WHILE, NEARBY, YOUNG CONAN WASTES FEW PRECIOUS MOMENTS TRYING TO FATHOM THE MYSTERIES OF *TIME AND SPACE*...

...BUT CONTINUES TO TEST THE *BARS* OF HIS MAKESHIFT PRISON.

AND STILL THE VISIONS *DANCE MADLY ON*... REVEALING MAN HURLED BACK INTO AN AGE OF STONE, AND BEGINNING ANEW HIS SLOW, UPWARD *CLIMB*...

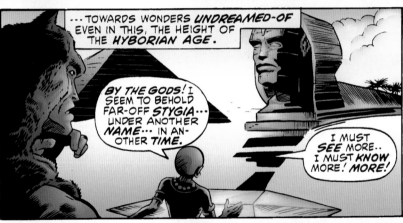

...TOWARDS WONDERS *UNDREAMED-OF* EVEN IN THIS, THE HEIGHT OF THE *HYBORIAN AGE*.

BY THE GODS! I SEEM TO BEHOLD FAR-OFF *STYGIA*... UNDER ANOTHER *NAME*... IN ANOTHER *TIME*.

I MUST *SEE* MORE.. I MUST *KNOW* MORE! MORE!

STOP, OLD MAN! YOU ARE GOING ...*TOO FAR!*

WE WERE NOT *MEANT* TO LOOK ON THINGS LIKE THIS.. *BEFORE THEIR TIME.*

BUT THE WIDE-EYED SHAMAN *HEEDS NOT*... AS THE IMAGE OF MAN'S *ULTIMATE CONQUEST* FLOODS THE PIT-DARK CHAMBER... AND THE EARTH, THE CENTER OF PRIMITIVE MAN'S SMALL UNIVERSE, IS LEFT *FAR, FAR BEHIND!*

VOLFF... WHAT *MADNESS* IS THIS? THE STARS --*THE STARS*--!

THESE SIGHTS -- HAVE DRIVEN THE OLD MAN *MAD!*

AAAARRRRRR!

THEN, EVEN AS THAT CRY STILL ECHOES···

CONAN·· STOP!

YOU'LL BE SLAIN··!

THEN LET ME DIE A *WARRIOR'S DEATH*···

···NOT PENNED UP LIKE SOME *SHEEP* RIPE FOR *SLAUGHTER!*

THE CIMMERIAN HAS *BROKEN FREE!*

HE'S FAR *STRONGER* THAN WE THOUGHT. *KILL HIM*··!

MAYBE YOU *WILL*·· BUT FIRST, I'LL SEE YON STAR-STONE *SHATTERED.*

FROM ITS *DEPTHS,* I KNOW, CAME THE *WINGED DEVILS* WHICH SLEW THE VALIANT *OLAV*···

BUT YOU'LL CALL FORTH *NO MORE* FIENDS FROM BEYOND···

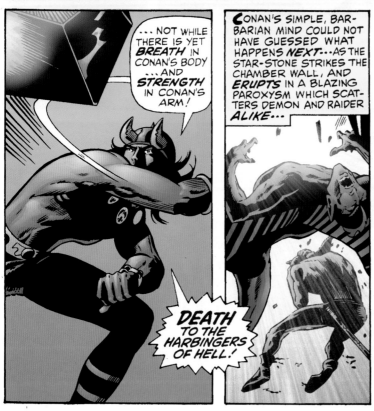

···NOT WHILE THERE IS YET *BREATH* IN CONAN'S BODY ···AND *STRENGTH* IN CONAN'S ARM!

*DEATH* TO THE HARBINGERS OF HELL!

CONAN'S SIMPLE, BAR-BARIAN MIND COULD NOT HAVE GUESSED WHAT HAPPENS *NEXT*···AS THE STAR-STONE STRIKES THE CHAMBER WALL, AND *ERUPTS* IN A BLAZING PAROXYSM WHICH SCAT-TERS DEMON AND RAIDER *ALIKE*···

···WHILE THE YOUNG CIMMERIAN SCOOPS UP THE LITHE FORM OF THE GIRL CALLED *TARA*··· AND FLEES IN MORTAL TERROR FOR *BOTH THEIR LIVES*···!

AND BEHIND THEM, THE *WINGED ONES* FADE SWIFTLY BACK INTO THAT DIM NETHERWORLD WHICH SPAWNED THEM, LIKE STRAWS CONSUMED BY A HOLOCAUST···

--- WHILE THE DYING *SHAMAN* SHOUTS UNAVAILING SPELLS INTO THE RAGING INFERNO···

···AND *VOLFF THE WILY* LEARNS AT LAST THAT ALL HIS TRICKERY HAS BUT LIGHTED HIS WAY TO *FLAMING DEATH*···

FOR, EVEN AS CONAN BEARS HIS LOVELY BURDEN INTO THE OPEN AIR, A FIERY *EXPLOSION* ROCKS THE CAVERN BEHIND THEM!

YOU *FOOL*···· YOU BARBARIAN FOOL··· YOU HAVE *DOOMED* ME···

*CURSE* THE MOMENT OF WEAKNESS WHEN I FELT *PITY* FOR YOU!

*DOOMED?* NAY, YOU'RE *SAFE* NOW··· OUT OF THAT MADMAN'S *CLUTCHES!*

YOU STILL··· DO NOT *COMPREHEND.* BUT YOU *SHALL*··· IN A FEW FLEETING MOMENTS···

WHAT ARE YOU *RAVING* ABOUT, WOMAN?

HAVE I *SAVED* YOU FROM THE FIRES WITHIN, ONLY TO HAVE YOU MOUTH *NONSEN--?*

*CROM'S DEVILS!*

WHAT VILE *SORCERY* IS THIS??

THE *FEMALE* I CARRIED FROM THE CAVE...

... IS CHANGED INTO ONE OF THE *WINGED DEMONS!*

SO *YOU*... WOULD CALL ME, MORTAL...

NOT LONG AGO... THE OLD *SHAMAN* WHISKED ME... FROM MY UNIVERSE *WITHIN* THE SHATTERED STAR-STONE...

... TRANSFORMED ME INTO AN EARTHLY *HANDMAID,* TO LIGHT HIS LONELY DAYS.

BUT HE COULD NOT KEEP ME HERE *FOR-E'ER*... UNLESS *ANOTHER* TOOK MY PLACE... IN MY DISTANT WORLD...

AND THAT OTHER WAS TO BE... *CONAN?*

AY... AND SO YOU KNOW AT LAST... THE SECRET OF THE CEREMONY OF *TRANSFERRAL.*

BUT NOW... MY *OWN* COSMOS CALLS ME... TO ENDURE ETERNALLY THE HELLISH *FLAMES* WHICH FLICKER THERE.

FARE THEE WELL, MORTAL... AND RECALL ONE DAY... THAT *TARA* FOUND YOU FAIR...

WONDER UPON *WONDER!*

THE WINGED ONE IS *GONE*... TO WORLDS WHERE NO MAN CAN *FOLLOW.*

*T*HEN, THERE IS NO MORE NEED FOR *SPOKEN WORDS,* FOR NONE ARE LEFT ALIVE TO HEAR THEM. SMOKE POURS FROM THE SHAMAN'S CAVERN, DARK HERALD OF THE *DEATH* THAT ALL WITHIN HAVE DIED...

NIGHT-WINGED *THOUGHTS* FLIT ACROSS CONAN'S BRAIN ... *MEMORIES* OF THE DREAD DEEDS OF THE DAY JUST DONE... THE SLAYING OF A VALIANT FRIEND... THE MARVELS OF AN INVISIBLE WORLD REVEALED... IMAGES OF MANY-TOWERED CITIES AND DYING CONTINENTS AND... AND...

... AND *KINGS!* AYE, WASN'T THERE SOMETHING ABOUT A KINGDOM? A VISION OF CONAN AS *MONARCH* OF SOME UNGUESSED-AT LAND?

BUT ALREADY THE IMAGE *FADES*...TOO LONG AGO AND TOO FANTASTIC TO TROUBLE THE MIND OF A YOUTH WHO HAS NEITHER DAGGER NOR VENISON TO SUSTAIN HIM.

THE MOON IS A WHITE, WATCHING EYE... THE JOURNEY HOME IS HARD... AND THERE ARE NO REALITIES WORTH THE WISHING, SAVE *FOOD* AND A FINELY WROUGHT *SWORD.*

[FINIS]

# LAIR OF THE BEAST-MEN!

IT IS SUMMER IN THE NORTH-LYING KINGDOM CALLED *AESGAARD,* HERE IN THIS WORLD OF MORE THAN ONE HUNDRED CENTURIES AGO--- BUT STILL A BLANKET OF *SNOW AND ICE* RESTS HEAVY UPON THE LAND--- AS A DARK-HAIRED YOUTH KNEELS GRIMLY BEFORE A *SHAGGY FORM* WHICH, MERE MOMENTS BEFORE, HAD TRIED TO *SNUFF OUT* HIS BRIEF LIFE ---

THE GIANT ONE IS *DEAD...*

--- BECAUSE HE THOUGHT ME TOO *SMALL,* TOO PUNY TO *FIGHT BACK.*

BUT, WHAT MANNER OF MAN OR BRUTE *IS* IT THAT CAME CHARGING TOWARD ME FROM OUT OF *NOWHERE?*

STAN LEE EDITOR • ROY THOMAS WRITER • BARRY SMITH ARTIST • SAL BUSCEMA INKER • SAM ROSEN LETTERER • BASED ON THE HERO CREATED BY ROBERT E. HOWARD

WELL THEN, I SUPPOSE I *MUST* PURSUE HER—

IF NOTHING ELSE, SHE DOUBTLESS *DWELLS* NEAR HERE—AND IT'S NOT GETTING ANY *WARMER.*

*HALT,* WOMAN—NO NEED TO *FLEE.*

UPON MY WORD, I WANT NOTHING FROM YOU BUT *DIRECTIONS*... OR AT MOST, A NIGHT'S *LODGINGS.*

*LODGINGS?* AYE, WE'LL GIVE YOU LODGINGS IN *BRUTHEIM,* LONG-HAIR—

—FOR THE REST OF YOUR UNHAPPY *LIFE!*

*AAARRAAA*

*WELL MET,* ZHA-GORR—THE BARBARIAN GOES *DOWN.*

BUT ONLY AT THE COST OF MY CHOICEST *PIKE,* MOIRA. HOW *STRONG* HE MUST—

*WHAT?* HE *STILL* MOVES?

*LOOK* AT HIM, MOIRA—HOW HE *GROPES* FOR ME, EVEN THRU HALF-DAZED EYES.

HE'LL MAKE A *WORTHY* SLAVE—AND THAT FOR *CERTAIN!*

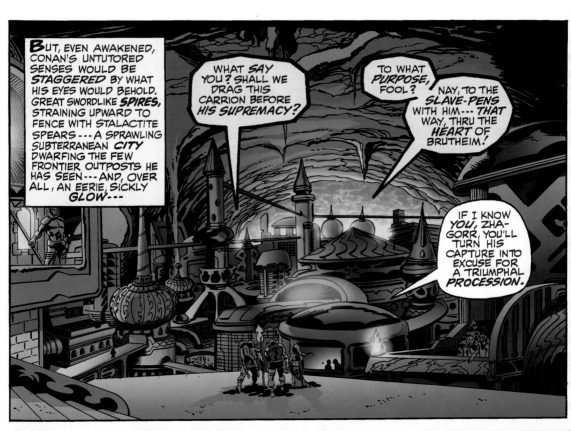

BUT, EVEN AWAKENED, CONAN'S UNTUTORED SENSES WOULD BE *STAGGERED* BY WHAT HIS EYES WOULD BEHOLD. GREAT SWORDLIKE *SPIRES*, STRAINING UPWARD TO FENCE WITH STALACTITE SPEARS --- A SPRAWLING SUBTERRANEAN *CITY* DWARFING THE FEW FRONTIER OUTPOSTS HE HAS SEEN --- AND, OVER ALL, AN EERIE, SICKLY *GLOW* ---

WHAT *SAY* YOU? SHALL WE DRAG THIS CARRION BEFORE *HIS SUPREMACY*?

TO WHAT *PURPOSE*, FOOL?

NAY, TO THE *SLAVE-PENS* WITH HIM --- *THAT* WAY, THRU THE *HEART* OF BRUTHEIM!

IF I KNOW *YOU*, ZHA-GORR, YOU'LL TURN HIS CAPTURE INTO EXCUSE FOR A TRIUMPHAL *PROCESSION*.

AND WHY SHOULD I *NOT*, FEMALE?

IS NOT *ZHA-GORR* MIGHTIEST OF ALL HIS SUPREMACY'S *GUARDSMEN*?

IS NOT *MY* NAME VOICED MORE LOUDLY AT THE *GAMES* THAN ANY SAVE THAT OF THE *KING* HIMSELF?

THEN, HIS BRAIN STILL REELING, THE BLACK-MANED BARBARIAN IS SEARCHED --- *SHACKLED* --- AND HURLED HEADLONG INTO A CLAMMY, BENIGHTED CHAMBER ---

IN *THERE*, MANLING! LANGUISH WITH THE *REST* OF YOUR LOATHSOME KIND.

≡ PHAAUGH! ≡ ALREADY I GROW *ILL* FROM THE *MAN-REEK* HERE.

SO, OUR MASTERS' NETS HAVE SNARED *ONE MORE* LUCKLESS TRAVELER.

HO, FELLOW. I AM *KIORD*, CHIEF THRALL OF BRUT-HEIM BARRACKS.

I AM *CONAN*, A CIMMERIAN. BUT--- HAVE I BEEN CAST AMONG *SPECTRES?* YOU ARE ALL---SO *PALE*.

AS *YOU* SHALL BE, YOUTH, WHEN YOU HAVE DWELT A WHILE IN THE *LAND OF ALWAYS-LIGHT*.

WE HAVE HEARD OF SOMETHING IN THE OUTER WORLD CALLED THE *SUN*, WHICH TURNS THE SKIN TO *BRONZE*.

BUT WE HAVE NEVER *SEEN* IT... NOR SHALL *YOU*, EVER AGAIN.

*NO?* THEN SLAY ME *NOW* WITH THOSE GREAT HANDS, TALL ONE---

---FOR, I *WILL* BE *FREE!!*

CONAN---*HOLD!* YOU DO NOT *UNDERSTAND!*

*NOW* DO YOU SEE? I MEANT ONLY THAT *METAL BARS* HOLD YOU PRISONER---MAKE YOU *ONE* OF US.

ALAS, WE ALL WERE *BORN* SLAVES---BUT *YOU*, TOO, SHALL *GROW OLD* AS ONE.

*BORN* A SLAVE? OF THOSE BRUTISH *BEAST-MEN* BELOW?

YOU WERE *RIGHT*, KIORD. I DO *NOT* UNDERSTAND.

"THEN *HEARKEN*, MAN-LING FROM THE WORLD BEYOND···

"*LISTEN*, AND I'LL TELL YOU A TALE HANDED DOWN FROM CHIEF *THRALL* TO CHIEF *THRALL*, SINCE TIME OUT OF MIND.

"LONG, LONG AGO, IN THAT OUTER WORLD WHICH WE HAVE NEVER GLIMPSED, A HUMAN *WANDERER* FROM AFAR LED A SMALL *WAR-PARTY* INTO THE ICY WASTES WHICH LIE ABOVE OUR HEADS.

"THEIR *MISSION*···TO *DESTROY* THE RUMORED BEAST-MEN, ERE THEY GREW STRONG ENOUGH TO MENACE THE WORLD WHERE *MEN* RULE···

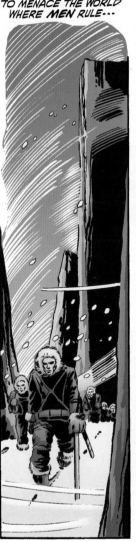

" BUT, THOSE BOLD WARRIORS WERE FATED *NEVER TO RETURN* TO THE HAUNTS OF MEN.

"*AMBUSHED*···SORELY *OUTNUMBERED*···THEY WERE *DEFEATED*···

"··· YET, NOT *SLAIN*··· NO, NOT *ALL*··· FOR, THE BEAST-MEN WERE SHREWD, AND LEARNED FROM THE CAPTIVES OF SOMETHING CALLED··· A *WEAPON*.

" THEY *ALSO* FOUND THAT MEN MADE *GOOD WORKERS*···

"··· *TOO* GOOD, IN FACT, TO BE ALLOWED TO *DIE OUT* WHEN THEIR MEAGRE LIFESPAN WAS DONE···

"··· NOT SO LONG AS THERE WERE HUMAN *FEMALES* DWELLING ON THE EDGES OF THE ICE-WASTES···

"··· WHO WOULD MAKE LOVELY *BRIDES* FOR THEIR HAPLESS *MAN-SLAVES*···*!*

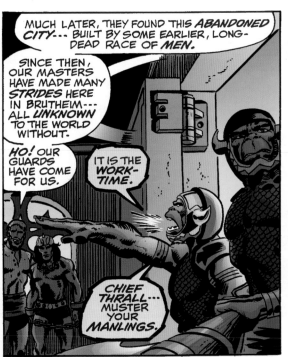

MUCH LATER, THEY FOUND THIS *ABANDONED CITY*··· BUILT BY SOME EARLIER, LONG-DEAD RACE OF *MEN.*

SINCE THEN, OUR MASTERS HAVE MADE MANY *STRIDES* HERE IN BRUTHEIM--- ALL *UNKNOWN* TO THE WORLD *WITHOUT.*

*HO!* OUR GUARDS HAVE COME FOR US.

IT IS THE *WORK-TIME.*

CHIEF THRALL··· MUSTER YOUR MANLINGS.

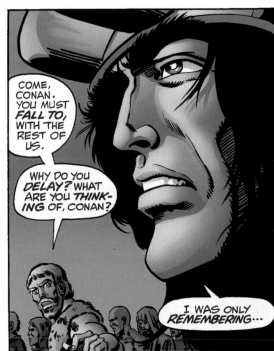

COME, CONAN. YOU MUST *FALL TO,* WITH THE REST OF US.

WHY DO YOU *DELAY?* WHAT ARE YOU *THINK-ING* OF, CONAN?

I WAS ONLY *REMEMBERING*···

---THAT THE NAME *"CHIEF THRALL"* STILL MEANS---A *SLAVE.*

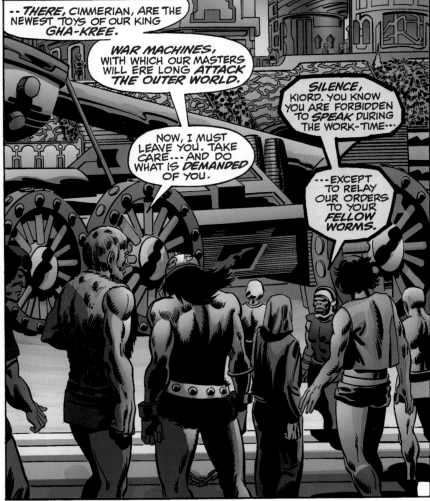

--*THERE,* CIMMERIAN, ARE THE NEWEST TOYS OF OUR KING *GHA-KREE.*

*WAR MACHINES,* WITH WHICH OUR MASTERS WILL ERE LONG *ATTACK* THE OUTER WORLD.

NOW, I MUST *LEAVE* YOU. TAKE CARE··· AND DO WHAT IS *DEMANDED* OF YOU.

*SILENCE,* KIORD. YOU KNOW YOU ARE FORBIDDEN TO *SPEAK* DURING THE WORK-TIME···

---EXCEPT TO RELAY OUR ORDERS TO YOUR *FELLOW WORMS.*

THEN, CONAN STANDS ALONE... *IN CHAINS* FOR THE FIRST TIME OF HIS YOUNG LIFE, AND NOT AT ALL *LIKING* IT...

HO THERE, DOG!

AHH, MANLING... THE *FIRE* IN YOUR EYES TELLS ME YOU *REMEMBER* ZHA-GORR... THE ONE WHO *CAPTURED* YOU.

YES... I REMEMBER. AND I AM A *MAN*, NOT A "MANLING!"

HOLD YOUR TONGUE, FOOL. YOU WERE NOT ASKED A *QUESTION.*

HAH! THIS WAR-HELM IS NOT FOR THE LIKES OF A *SLAVE*... I CLAIM IT FOR MY *PRIZE.*

WHAT SAY YOU TO *THAT,* DOG?

THIS TIME, CONAN'S COBRA-QUICK ANSWER COMES NOT IN *WORDS*...

GRROKKK

BUT, HIS HEAVY CHAINS *HAMPER* HIM... AND THE *SMALLER* OF THE TWO MAN-APES WIELDS HIS PIKE MUCH MORE *SWIFTLY* THAN CONAN COULD HAVE GUESSED...

GOOD TIMING, HAR-LANN. I HAD FORGOTTEN THAT SLAVES TAKEN FROM THE *OUTER WORLD* OFTEN HAVE SOME *FIGHT* LEFT IN THEM.

TOO *MUCH* FIGHT. I SAY WE SHOULD KNOCK IT *OUT* OF HIM.

*UH OH!* THE NEW ONE IS AS GOOD AS *DEAD* NOW. I HOPE THEY DON'T TAKE HIS ACTIONS OUT ON *US,* AS WELL.

THE BARBARIAN STRUGGLES TO HIS *FEET*... KNOWING HE'LL BE *STRUCK DOWN* AGAIN.

IS *THAT* THE DIFFERENCE BETWEEN A *MANLING*... AND A *MAN?*

STAND UP *STRAIGHT*, DOG! HOW CAN I PUT MY *PIKE* THRU YOU TILL YOU DO?

*HOLD!* WHAT ARE YOU *DOING* THERE?

ZHA-GORR ---IT'S *HIS SUPREMACY* ---WITH HIS *HANDMAID MOIRA*.

I WAS TEACHING THIS MANLING A *LESSON*, SIRE, ERE I *SKEWER* HIM LIKE A PIG.

HMMM--- IT IS CLEAR THIS ONE WILL *NEVER* MAKE A GOOD SLAVE... BUT STILL IT IS A SHAME TO *WASTE* HIS *DEATH*.

REMOVE THESE *CHAINS*, AND WE'LL *SEE* WHO LEARNS THE LESSON.

MAY I *SUGGEST*, SIRE---THE *GAMES!?*

AYE... THE *GAMES* IT SHALL BE! BY MY *CROWN*, MADE FROM THE TEETH OF THE LONG-DEAD *TUSK-BEARS*---

WE'LL SEE YOU *GROVEL* BEFORE YOU DIE, MANLING!

THERE IS *NO NIGHT* IN BRUTHEIM, WHERE PHOSPHORESCENT NUGGETS STUD THE JAGGED CAVERN WALLS---

YET, IT IS EVER *DARK* IN THE SLAVE BARRACKS WHERE, LATER, CONAN SITS BROODING--- AND HEARS A STEALTHY *FOOTFALL*---

WHO *GOES* THERE?

YOUR EARS ARE *SHARP*, CONAN. FEAR NOT---IT IS ONLY I, *KIORD*.

YOU MOVE *SOFTLY*, FOR ONE SO LARGE. BUT WHY DO YOU *SEEK* ME OUT?

I---HAVE *BROUGHT* YOU SOMETHING.

IT IS BUT A *KNIFE OF OBSIDIAN* WHICH I CARVED LONG AGO WITH STONES.

I MEANT IT TO TAKE MY *OWN* LIFE, IF EVER NEED AROSE... BUT IT WILL SAVE *YOU* SUFFERING, AS WELL.

YOU GAVE ME THIS BLADE --- SO I COULD *KILL MYSELF?*

OF COURSE. WHY *ELSE?*

NEVER MIND. I'LL FIND *SOME* USE FOR IT.

BUT TELL ME, KIORD--- WITH YOUR STRENGTH AND SKILL, WHY DO YOU NOT LEAD A *REVOLT* AGAINST YOUR BEAST-MEN MASTERS?

*I?* NAY, WE WERE BORN AND BRED TO *SERVE*... AND SERVE WE *SHALL.*

ANY OTHER COURSE MUST LEAD TO *BLOOD SHED*, AND I WOULD NOT SEE *ANY* OF MY *FLOCK* SHED SO MUCH AS A *DROP.*

PERHAPS *BLOOD* IS A *PRICE* YOU MUST PAY... TO BE *FREE.*

*NO, I SAY!* I'M NO *COWARD*... AYE, WE KNOW THAT WORD DOWN *HERE*, TOO.

BUT YOUR PRICE IS TOO HIGH-- *TOO HIGH!*

BETTER TO LIVE OUT OUR LIVES AS *SLAVES*, THAN ALL TO *DIE*--- ON THE ALTAR OF SOME *DREAMER'S FOLLY.*

CONAN--- I, *TOO*, HAVE DREAMED OF BEING FREE.

OFTEN IN THE DARKNESS I HAVE DREAMED THAT OUR MASTERS HAVE SIMPLY *VANISHED*---

--- AND THAT I *RULED* THIS CITY, AS ITS KIND AND LOVING *KING.*

BUT THERE WAS *NO BLOOD* ON THE PAVEMENT, CONAN, *NO BLOOD!*

THEN *DREAM ON*, MANLING--- TILL THE DAY YOU *DIE.*

SOMEONE ONCE TOLD ME *I* WOULD BE A KING, TOO--- I FORGET *WHO.*

BUT WHEN *I* SLEEP, I HAVE *NO DREAMS.*

GOOD NIGHT. MY *THANKS* FOR THE KNIFE.

THE **GAMES OF GHA-KREE** --- EVENT SUPREME OF **BRUTHEIM** --- THE SOLE TIME WHEN ARE GATHERED **ALL** THE BEAST-MEN WHO LORD IT OVER THIS SMALL BUT SAVAGE REALM --- AND WHERE NOW ARE DISPLAYED THE GREAT **WEAPONS OF WAR** WHICH SOON SHALL CARVE THEM OUT AN **EMPIRE** FROM THE WORLD ABOVE.

THE **MANLINGS** WATCH, TOO, PENNED IN WOODEN CAGES --- FOR HERE THE BEAST-MEN **EXECUTE**, IN TRIAL-BY-COMBAT, THOSE HUMANS THEY DEEM MOST **REBELLIOUS** --- AND THUS MOST **DANGEROUS** ---

I DREAMED MY **DREAM** AGAIN, WIFE -- BUT IT WAS **DIFFERENT** THIS TIME -- AND THE BARBARIAN **CONAN** WAS THERE.

QUIET, KIORD. DO YOU WISH TO **SHARE** HIS FATE?

I WOULD BE **PROUD** TO --- IF PRIDE WERE **MINE** TO KNOW!

CONAN!

WE HAVE CRINGED, EVER SINCE THE HOUR OF OUR **BIRTH**.

SHOW US HOW TO **DIE** --- THAT PERHAPS WE SHALL LEARN HOW TO **LIVE**.

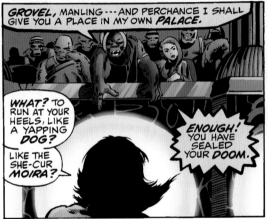

GROVEL, MANLING --- AND PERCHANCE I SHALL GIVE YOU A PLACE IN MY OWN **PALACE**.

**WHAT?** TO RUN AT YOUR HEELS, LIKE A YAPPING **DOG**?

LIKE THE SHE-CUR **MOIRA**?

**ENOUGH!** YOU HAVE SEALED YOUR **DOOM**.

RELEASE THE **LION!**

AYE, GREAT SIRE.

LIKE ALL BARBARIANS, YOUNG CONAN HAS HEARD *LEGENDS* OF THE DREADED *SNOW-LION*--- BUT IN HIS FEW YEARS, HE HAS NEVER BEFORE *SEEN* ONE.

THE BRUTE'S ROAR DOES ITS WORK. FOR A MOMENT, THE CIMMERIAN STANDS TRANSFIXED WITH *FEAR*--- BUT *ONLY* FOR A MOMENT.

FOR, IS NOT THIS AT LEAST A *NATURAL* FOE--- FAR MORE NATURAL THAN THE GROTESQUE BEAST-MEN WHO *GLARE DOWN* AT HIM?

HE DRAWS HIS *BLADE* FROM HIDING ---AND HE *WAITS*---

--- NOR MUST HE WAIT FOR *LONG!*

HOT, FETID *BREATH*--- A RUSH OF *AIR* DISPLACED BY A MASSIVE FORM--- THE SENSE OF STEEL-MUSCLED *DEATH* HURTLING BY---

AND *BACK* AGAIN---!

SUDDENLY, A LAST AND *DESPERATE* SURGE OF STRENGTH--- POWERFUL YOUNG SINEWS STRETCHED TO THE *BREAKING POINT*---

AND THEN--- FROM DESPAIR, *TRIUMPH!* FROM DEFEAT--- *VICTORY!*

--- AND FROM OUT OF THE JAWS OF DEATH---*LIFE!*

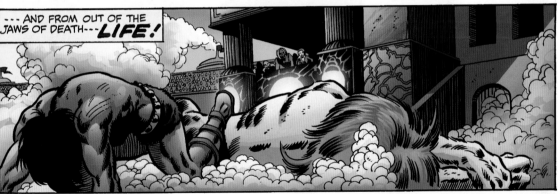

THE MANLING HAD A *WEAPON!* IT IS *FORBIDDEN!*

FOR THAT HE SHALL DIE *SLOWLY*---AND WISH THE GREAT CAT'S *TALONS* HAD FOUND HIS HEART.

GUARDS-MEN!

IT SEEMS ALL *UN-REAL* TO CONAN AS HE STARES OUT THRU HALF-DAZED EYES---

---TO DIE IN A HALF-LIGHTED *ARENA*, IN SOME SUNKEN *CAVERN* ---PUT TO THE SWORD BY *APES* THAT WALK LIKE *MEN*.

WHAT CONAN'S MIND CANNOT *ACCEPT*... CONAN'S BODY WILL NOT *YIELD* TO. SQUINTING THRU DIMMED EYES, HE *LASHES OUT*...

-- BUT *TOO LATE!*

HAH! FRIEND *ZHA-GORR* WILL BE SORRY HE WORKS THE *OTHER* END OF THE ARENA TODAY---

--WHEN *I* DELIVER THE *DEATH-STROKE.*

HALT, HAR-LANN. IT IS *HIS SUPREMACY* WHO MUST DECREE THE MANLING'S FATE.

DEATH!

BUT NOT UNTIL HE *BEGS* IT-- TILL A SWORD THRUST IS HIS MOST FERVENT *PRAYER.*

NOT BEFORE HE GROANS THAT HE IS A *MANLING* SHALL HE DIE LIKE A *DOG.*

NO! YOU HAVE TURNED *US* INTO DOGS--- INTO *LESS* THAN ANIMALS.

YOU *WON'T* DO THE SAME TO HIM. YOU *WON'T!*

HUSBAND-- *HUSH!* REMEMBER YOUR *DREAM*--

*TOO LONG* HAVE I BEEN THRALL TO A *DREAM* ---AS MUCH AS TO THE *BEAST-MEN.*

FROM THIS HOUR, I SHALL BE SLAVE TO *NEITHER.*

FROM THIS HOUR, LET THERE BE NO MORE MANLINGS...

--- BUT ONLY FREE MEN--- AND DEAD MEN!

WELL? WHAT ARE YOU WAITING FOR?

THEN, THE DAM BREAKS-- AND A TORRENT OF TERRIFIED HUMANITY POURS THRU THE SHATTERED DOOR---

---MOST TO FLEE... BUT A FEW, DESPITE THEIR FEARS, TO FIGHT UNARMED...!

THIS ISN'T AS HOPELESS AS IT APPEARS, BARBARIAN.

OUR MASTERS ARE LIKE SHEEP. IF WE CAN BEST THE GUARDSMEN, THE REST KNOW NOT HOW TO FIGHT.

THEN DON'T WASTE BREATH ON WORDS, FRIEND...

--- BUT STRIKE OUT AT OUR FOES, AND SELL YOUR LIFE DEARLY IF YOU MUST.

GUARDS! PROTECT YOU THE WAR-WEAPONS!

YES.. THE WEAPONS!

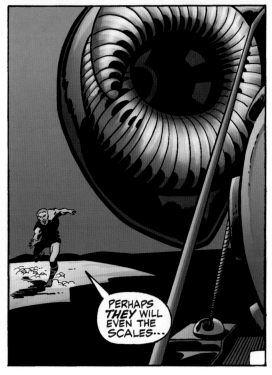

PERHAPS THEY WILL EVEN THE SCALES...

--- WHILE THERE STILL IS *TIME.*

*KIORD!* WHAT ARE YOU TRYING TO *DO?*

DON'T YOU *SEE,* CONAN, WHERE THIS RAM IS *AIMED?*

OF *COURSE!* IT FACES-- THE *BEAST-KING* AND HIS HAIRY COURT.

THOSE WITHOUT WHOM THE MAN-APES CANNOT *STAND.*

*AYE...* BUT THE GREAT WHEELS --TURN *HARD..*

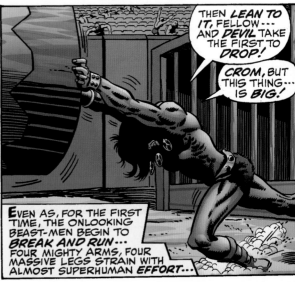

THEN *LEAN TO IT,* FELLOW--- AND *DEVIL* TAKE THE FIRST TO *DROP!*

*CROM,* BUT THIS THING... IS *BIG!*

*EVEN AS,* FOR THE FIRST TIME, THE ONLOOKING BEAST-MEN BEGIN TO *BREAK AND RUN*--- FOUR MIGHTY ARMS, FOUR MASSIVE LEGS STRAIN WITH ALMOST SUPERHUMAN *EFFORT...*

*AND,* THE RAM BEGINS TO *MOVE,* INCH---

IT'S *GOING,* CONAN! IT'S *GOING!*

-- BY AGONIZING *INCH* ---

THEN *HARDER,* MAN--- *HARDER!*

--- UNTIL SUDDENLY, WITH A THUNDEROUS *ROAR* THAT SHAKES THE EARTH TO BITS ---

NO! NNOOOOOOOOOOOO

---AND WHO COULD HAVE GUESSED THAT THOSE FEW CRUMBLING *PILLARS* FORMED THE SUPPORT FOR THE VERY *ARENA* ITSELF?

WE HAVE WON! WE ARE FREE!

*HO!* HERE'S MY *HELMET,* WHERE ZHA-GORR MUST HAVE *DROPPED* IT.

WELL, YOUR DREAM HAS COME TO *PASS,* KIORD--AND PRECIOUS *LITTLE* OF MEN'S BLOOD HAS BEEN SHED. WHAT THINK YOU OF *THAT?*

KIORD?

SAVE YOUR *BREATH,* MANLING! I KNOW NOT HOW IT IS IN THE *WORLD ABOVE*---

BUT IN BRUTHEIM, *DEAD MEN* DO NOT *SPEAK!*

KIORD!

43

I PRAY YOU HAVE A **SOUL**, ZHA-GORR---

---THAT IT MAY **DRIFT** AND **MUTTER** **FOREVER** IN SOME **BEAST-MAN'S** **HELL!**

WE ARE **FREE**... FREE TO BE OUR **OWN** MASTERS AT LAST--THANKS BE TO YOU AND **KIORD**, BARBARIAN.

BUT--- **KIORD** LIES SO **STILL**. IS HE---?

**T**HE LAST MAN-APES ARE **GONE** NOW-- FLED, UNCOMPREHENDING, TO DARK FORGOTTEN **CAVERNS** AND PERHAPS TO THE SNOW-LANDS WHICH SPAWNED THEIR **ANCESTORS** ---AS **TEARS** WELL UP IN EYES WHICH HAVE NEVER KNOWN THEM ---

**BACK**, I SAY. **STAND ASIDE!**

THERE IS SOMETHING I MUST **SEEK OUT** IN THESE CRUMPLED RUINS---

AND--- I HAVE **FOUND** IT.

**YES**, THRALLS --- YOU **ARE** FREE NOW, AND LONG MAY YOU **REMAIN** SO.

BUT LET YOUR **LEGENDS** SAY OF THIS DAY THAT A **KING** LED YOU TO VICTORY---

--- AND THAT HIS NAME WAS **KIORD.**

FOR HE WAS THE **LAST** OF THE MANLINGS---

BUT **FIRST** AMONG--- **MEN.**

*Finis*

44

FROM OUT OF EARTH'S DIM, FORGOTTEN PAST·· FROM THE CENTURIES WHICH SPRAWL BETWEEN THE SINKING OF ATLANTIS AND THE DAWNING OF HISTORY·· COMES··

# CONAN THE BARBARIAN! ™

## THE TWILIGHT OF THE GRIM GREY GOD!

NIGHT IN HYPERBOREA··· THAT RUDE, FIERCE LAND WHICH ONCE WAS FIRST AMONG HYBORIAN KINGDOMS, BUT NOW IS SUNKEN BACK INTO SAVAGERY AND BARBARISM.

A VOICE ECHOES AMONG THE BLACK REACHES OF THE REARING MOUNTAINS··· AND AT ITS SEPULCHRAL SOUND, CONAN WHEELS, SNARLING LIKE A WOLF AT BAY···

CROM'S DEVILS! WHO'S THAT? IF IT'S SOME HYPERBOREAN DOG, COME TO SKEWER ME BEFORE I CAN BREAK MY CHAINS, I'LL···

STAN ROY BARRY
LEE•THOMAS•SMITH
EDITOR WRITER ARTIST

SAL BUSCEMA —
EMBELLISHER
SAM ROSEN — LETTERER

FREELY ADAPTED FROM ROBERT E. HOWARD'S STORY "THE GREY GOD PASSES!"

BUT NOW, *SILENCE* HANGS HEAVY ON THE STARS ONCE MORE -- AND SO CONAN DRAWS *NEARER* THE TALL STRANGER HE HAS ESPIED...

WELL, CONAN -- YOU ARE *FAR* FROM YOUR NATIVE CIMMERIA.

I DO NOT *KNOW* YOU.. BUT IF YOU'VE COME TO TRY TO TAKE ME *BACK*...

WHITHER DO YOU *FLEE*, WITH HYPER-BOREAN *CHAINS* ABOUT YOUR WRISTS?

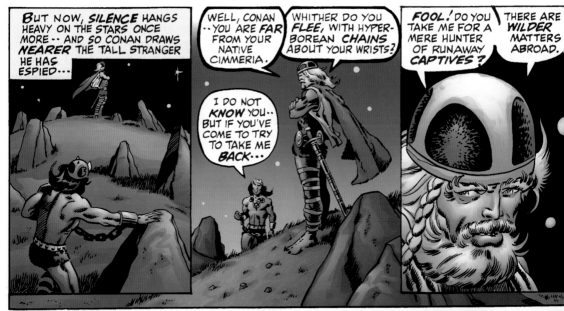

*FOOL!* DO YOU TAKE ME FOR A MERE *HUNTER* OF RUNAWAY *CAPTIVES?*

THERE ARE *WILDER* MATTERS ABROAD.

CAN'T YOU *SMELL* IT, CONAN? THE SCENT OF *BLOOD* IS ON THE WIND...

THE MUSK OF *SLAUGHTER* ...AND THE SHOUTS OF THE *SLAYING!*

THERE IS *WAR* ALONG THE BORDERS, STRIPLING. THE SPEARS OF *HYPER-BOREA* ARE RISING AGAINST THE SWORDS OF *BRYTHUNIA!*

THE *DEATH-FIRES* SOON SHALL LIGHT THE LAND LIKE THE MID-DAY *SUN.*

HOW CAN *YOU* KNOW THIS? WE ARE *LEAGUES* FROM THE BORDER.

WHO *ARE* YOU-- THAT YOU WIELD A BATTERED YET GLEAM-ING *SWORD?*

*TELL* ME, OR I'LL TAKE THESE CHAINS IN *HAND*, AND..

*WHAT??* YOU.. WOULD THREATEN *ME!?*

LIFT YOUR *EYES*, BOY.. AND LEARN TO WHOM YOU *SPEAK!*

AND NOW, THE CIMMERIAN *CRIES OUT* -- AS, FROM OUT THE BILLOWING CLOUDS ABOVE, WITH A GREAT RUSHING OF WIND, SWEEP *TWELVE SHAPES.*

AS IN A NIGHTMARE, CONAN BEHOLDS THE TWELVE *WINGED HORSES* AND THEIR RIDERS -- *WOMEN* IN FLOWING SILVER GARMENTS, THEIR GOLDEN HAIR STREAMING BEHIND THEM --- THEIR COLD *EYES* FIXED ON SOME AWESOME GOAL BEYOND HIS KEN.

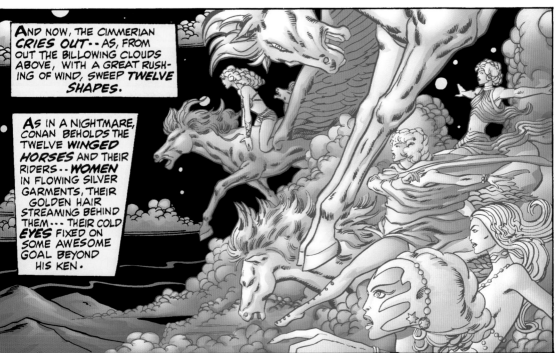

**THE CHOOSERS OF THE SLAIN!**

NOW COMES THE REAPING OF *KINGS* --- THE GARNERING OF *CHIEFS* LIKE A HARVEST.

TO EACH *BEING,* THERE IS AN APPOINTED *TIME* ---

-- AND EVEN THE GODS MUST *DIE.!!*

YOU COMPREHEND BUT *LITTLE* OF WHAT YOU HAVE SEEN AND HEARD, CONAN. YET, SOON YOU SHALL WITNESS THE PASSING OF *KINGS* -- AYE, AND OF *MORE* THAN KINGS!

NOW, GET YOU *GONE* -- FOR GIGANTIC *SHADOWS* STALK RED-HANDED ACROSS THE WORLD ---

AND *NIGHT* IS FALLING ON *HYPERBOREA.*

THEN, CONAN *FLEES*···BUT A LAST BACKWARD GLANCE SHOWS HIM THE STRANGER ETCHED AGAINST THE CLOUD-TORN SKY, CLOAK BLOWING IN THE WIND···

AND IT SEEMS TO CONAN THAT THE MAN HAS *GROWN* MONSTROUS IN STATURE, AND THAT HE LOOMS COLOSSAL AMONG THE CLOUDS··· AND THAT HE IS SUDDENLY *GREY* AS WITH VAST *AGE*.

···THE SUMMER GALE HAS BLOWN ITSELF OUT NOW, AND A LONE HORSEMAN RIDES IN SOMBER SILENCE···

PERHAPS HE THINKS OF THE MAMMOTH *CAMPSITE* NOT FAR DISTANT···OF 20,000 WARRIORS, MAKING DARK THE FACE OF THE FOREST.

PERHAPS HE THINKS OF THE COMING *BATTLE*··· AND OF THE *DEATHS* THAT MANY WILL DIE···AND PERHAPS HE IS JUST A TRIFLE AFRAID.

*HO* THERE, BRYTHUNIAN! REIN UP! I MUST *SPEAK* WITH YOU.

EH? WHO ARE *YOU*?

TELL ME-- HAS *BRYTHUNIA* GONE TO WAR WITH *HYPERBOREA*?

YOU DIDN'T ANSWER MY *QUESTION*, FELLOW···BUT YOUR *CHAINS* TELL ME YOU'VE LATELY BEEN IN HYPERBOREAN *SLAVE PENS*.

THEN-- YOU MUST TAKE ME *WITH* YOU··

AND THE ANSWER TO *YOUR* QUERY IS...*YES*!

···FOR, I HAVE MANY *HYPERBOREANS* TO KILL.

---BY CROM! FROM ALL YOU'VE TOLD ME, DUNLANG, IT'S JUST AS THE GREY MAN HINTED.

YET, HOW COULD HE HAVE KNOWN? SURELY IT WAS ALL A DREAM.

I GAVE YOU A RIDE ON A WHIM, BARBARIAN--- AND I STILL CAN'T BE SURE YOU WON'T TRY TO STAB ME IN THE BACK.

WHY NOT TELL ME HOW YOU CAME HERE--IF ONLY TO SET MY MIND AT EASE, EH?

"DONE, FRIEND. I WAS TRYING TO GET HOME AFTER A BATTLE WITH SOME-- APES-- WHEN HYPERBOREAN SLAVE TRADERS WAYLAID ME.

"THEY TOOK ME BACK TO THEIR LAND--AND THERE WAS A BLOND ONE WHO WAS HANDY WITH THE LASH.

"BUT ONE NIGHT, A GUARD WAS CARELESS---

"-- AND I FLED!

"THE BORDER OF YOUR KINGDOM WAS CLOSEST, SO I MADE FOR IT---

"-- HOPING, PERHAPS, TO MEET THAT BLOND ONE ALONG THE WAY."

WELL TOLD, MAN. YOU'VE A SCORE TO SETTLE WITH THAT SCUM, ALL RIGHT.

BUT THERE'S OUR CAMP BELOW.

DON'T GO BACK, DUNLANG! IF YOU VALUE YOUR LIFE... DON'T GO BACK!

WHO--?

EEVIN!

THEN.. YOU'VE NOT FORGOTTEN ME-- NOT EVEN HERE, WITH THE VULTURE OF WAR HOVERING BLACK IN THE AIR.

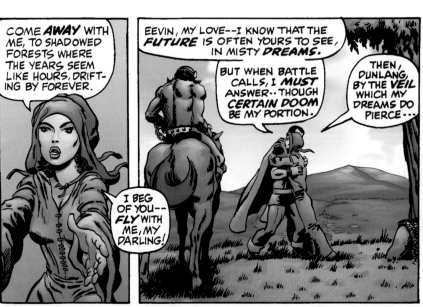

COME **AWAY** WITH ME, TO SHADOWED FORESTS WHERE THE YEARS SEEM LIKE HOURS, DRIFTING BY FOREVER.

I BEG OF YOU-- **FLY** WITH ME, MY DARLING!

EEVIN, MY LOVE--I KNOW THAT THE **FUTURE** IS OFTEN YOURS TO SEE, IN MISTY **DREAMS.**

BUT WHEN BATTLE CALLS, I **MUST** ANSWER..THOUGH **CERTAIN DOOM** BE MY PORTION.

THEN, DUNLANG, BY THE **VEIL** WHICH MY DREAMS DO PIERCE...

--YOU ARE AS GOOD AS **DEAD!**

WHILE, **ELSEWHERE** IN THE VAST WOOD, MIDWAY BETWEEN THE CAMPS OF BRYTHUNIAN AND HYPERBOREAN...

PLEASE, **MALACHI**... WE MET HERE TO SPEAK OF OUR **PLAN,** REMEMBER?

**BAH!** HOW CAN I THINK OF SCHEMES AND WARS, **KORMLADA** --WHEN YOUR PRESENCE BOILS MY BLOOD... **YOUR** LOVELINESS FILLS MY MIND?

NO, MALACHI. YOU KNOW THAT THE TIME GROWS **SHORT.**

**YES,** AND I AM COMMANDER OF THE **BRYTHUNIAN CAVALRY**--

--WHILE YOU ARE, **KING TOMAR'S WOMAN**--HE WHO IS WARLORD OF THE FIERCE **HYPERBOREANS.**

AND HAVE YOU CONSIDERED MY LORD'S **OFFER?**

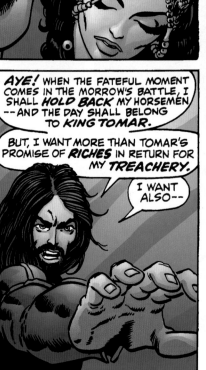

**AYE!** WHEN THE FATEFUL MOMENT COMES IN THE MORROW'S BATTLE, I SHALL **HOLD BACK** MY HORSEMEN --AND THE DAY SHALL BELONG TO **KING TOMAR.**

BUT, I WANT MORE THAN TOMAR'S PROMISE OF **RICHES** IN RETURN FOR MY **TREACHERY.**

I WANT ALSO--

--THE **KISS** OF A DEVIL-BORN **QUEEN!**

AND SO THEY *PART*-- THE BRYTHUNIAN *TRAITOR-TO-BE,* AND THE HAUGHTY, HIGH-BORN *KORMLADA*--!

--*AYE,* DUNLANG I *REPEAT* MY DREAD-ED WORDS.

IN MY DREAMS, I HAVE BEHELD YOU *DEAD*-- AND RINGED ABOUT WITH SHOUTING *WARRIORS.*

YET, I HAVE BROUGHT YOU A *GIFT* AGAINST THE TIME OF BATTLE.

IT *MAY* SAVE YOU-- BUT I HOPE *WITH-OUT* HOPE IN MY HEART.

A COAT OF-- *GOLDEN* MAIL?

AND *ENCHANTED* MAIL, TOO, IF I KNOW MY *EEVIN*-- WHOSE RACE WAS OLD WHEN THIS LAND WAS YOUNG.

THOUGH I HAVE ALWAYS DISDAINED ARMOR, I *SHALL* WEAR THIS-- FOR *YOUR* SAKE, IF NOT MY OWN.

NOW *COME,* CONAN -- IT IS TIME TO GO.

TAKE CARE, GREAT DUNLANG. BE NOT EVER IN THE *FORE-FRONT* OF TOMORROW'S CLASH.

FOR, OUR *FOES* ARE MAD WITH THE *LUST FOR CONQUEST*--

--AND I FEEL THE PRESENCE OF *GREY DEATH* HOVERING NEAR ME.

*ANOTHER* CAMP LIES BEYOND THE FOREST GREEN-- THE CAMP OF THE SAVAGE *HYPERBOREANS*-- AND WITHIN THIS CAMP, THE TENT OF THE HOT-BLOODED *KING TOMAR*---

KORMLADA!

*MUST* YOU BELLOW SO, TOMAR ?

I HAVE JUST *RE-TURNED* --FROM THE MISSION ON WHICH *YOU* YOUR-SELF SENT ME.

WELL THEN, **TELL** ME! WILL THE BRYTHUNIAN **MALACHI** WITHHOLD HIS CAVALRY... AND GIVE ME THE **VICTORY**?

YOU--ARE **HURTING** ME, MY LORD.

I'LL **BREAK** YOUR ARM, IF YOU DO NOT **TELL** ME--!

HE-- WILL DO AS YOU ASK--!

**GOOD.** I KNEW THE FOOL COULD BE **BOUGHT.**

NOW, BACK TO YOUR **KNITTING,** WOMAN--

I MUST MAKE READY FOR THE **BATTLE TO COME.**

AND WHEN THE BATTLE IS **DONE,** SWINE--AND THE **BRYTHUNIAN HOSTS** ARE SCATTERED...

I'LL PUT A **DAGGER** IN YOU-- AND SET UP **MALACHI** AS MY **PUPPET KING!**

-- MY HOME IS IN FAR-OFF **CIMMERIA,** DUNLANG. TELL ME, HOW DID THIS **BORDER WAR** BEGIN?

**KING TOMAR** AND OUR **KING BRIAN** HAVE BEEN ENEMIES FOR MORE YEARS THAN YOU HAVE **LIVED,** LAD.

BUT **HO!** THERE IS BRIAN'S **TENT.**

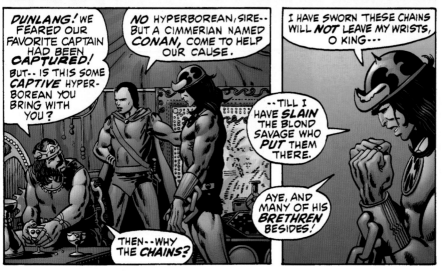

**DUNLANG!** WE FEARED OUR FAVORITE CAPTAIN HAD BEEN **CAPTURED!** BUT-- IS THIS SOME **CAPTIVE** HYPERBOREAN YOU BRING WITH YOU?

NO HYPERBOREAN, SIRE-- BUT A CIMMERIAN NAMED **CONAN,** COME TO HELP OUR CAUSE.

--TILL I HAVE **SLAIN** THE BLOND SAVAGE WHO **PUT** THEM THERE.

AYE, AND MANY OF HIS **BRETHREN** BESIDES!

I HAVE SWORN THESE CHAINS WILL **NOT** LEAVE MY WRISTS, O KING---

**WELL SPOKEN.** AND YOU'LL HAVE YOUR **CHANCE,** WHEN FIRE-FINGERED **DAWN** DRAWS NEAR.

THEN-- WHY THE **CHAINS?**

LATER, 'ROUND A ROARING CAMPFIRE---

YOU! BARBARIAN!

I AM *MALACHI*, CHIEF OF ALL THE KING'S *HORSEMEN*.

HE HAS ORDERED ME TO SEE THAT YOU PICK A *WEAPON* FOR THE COMING BATTLE, IF YOU WOULD *FIGHT* FOR US---

I DO *NOT* FIGHT FOR *YOU*, PIG-EYES-- BUT *AGAINST* THE HYPER-BOREANS.

AND I'LL DO IT *MY* WAY.

*INSULT* ME, WILL YOU, STRIPLING?

IF YOU WERE NOT UNDER *DUNLANG'S* PROTECTION, I'D--

THERE'S BUT *ONE* THING YOU YOU CAN DO FOR ME, PIG-EYES---

SLICE MY *CHAIN*-- HERE, WHERE I POINT.

NOW-- I *HAVE* MY WEAPON.

A HUNK OF RUSTING *CHAIN?* BAH--- YOU'LL BE THE *FIRST* TO FALL.

BUT-- IN THE END-- IT WILL MATTER *LITTLE*---

AND ALL THE NIGHT IS *GREY*-- AS GREY AS THAT GRIM, STARK *GIANT*, WHOSE WORDS STILL RING IN CONAN'S EARS---

"SOON YOU SHALL WITNESS THE PASSING OF *KINGS*-- AYE, AND OF *MORE* THAN KINGS!"

THEN, THRU THE MIST OF THE WHITENING DAWN..

---MEN MOVE LIKE GHOSTS, AND WEAPONS CLANK EERILY---

ARMOR-- TO FIGHT THAT HYPERBOREAN SCUM!

AS IF ARMOR WOULD STALL OFF *DEATH*, IF HE CALLED MY NAME!

WHERE'S YOUR *KING*? WHEN DOES HE COME FORTH TO *LEAD* US?

KING BRIAN? WE FIGHT FOR *HIM*-- NOT HE FOR *US*.

HE'LL COME FORTH FROM HIS TENT WHEN WE'VE *WON THE DAY* FOR HIM-- NOT *BEFORE*.

FARE THEE WELL, MY LOVE. IF WE DO NOT MEET AGAIN --

HUSH GIRL! WE'LL *LAUGH* OF THIS, WHEN NIGHT COMES AGAIN.

HORSEMEN, HO!

DUNLANG-- GATHER YOUR *HOSTS*-- ERE THE NORTHERN DOGS ARE *UPON* US!

AND SO THE *OLD* SEND FORTH THE *YOUNG* TO DIE-- WHILE *THEY* MAKE MERRY IN THEIR *TENTS*.

BACK IN CIMMERIA, OUR KINGS *LEAD* THE CHARGE--- THEIR *BROAD-SWORDS* IN THEIR HANDS.

MAYBE THAT'S BECAUSE WE'RE NOT... *CIVILIZED*.

NOR DOES EVEN THE TREACHEROUS *KING TOMAR* SKULK IN THE SAFETY OF HIS TENT.. BUT LEADS HIS WILD HORDE AS THE RAM LEADS THE FLOCK--

FOR BORRI! BORRI!!

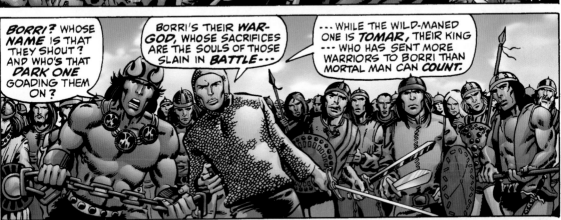

*BORRI?* WHOSE *NAME* IS THAT THEY SHOUT? AND WHO'S THAT *DARK ONE* GOADING THEM ON?

BORRI'S THEIR *WAR-GOD*, WHOSE SACRIFICES ARE THE SOULS OF THOSE SLAIN IN *BATTLE*---

---WHILE THE WILD-MANED ONE IS *TOMAR*, THEIR KING --- WHO HAS SENT MORE WARRIORS TO BORRI THAN MORTAL MAN CAN *COUNT.*

BUT NOW, THEY *CHARGE* --SO STAND YOU *FAST,* CIMMERIAN--

"..FOR THIS IS THE DAY THE RAVENS DRINK BLOOD!"

**A**ND NOW, A DEEP-TONED *ROAR* GOES UP TO THE HEAVENS--- AND TWO GREAT HOSTS ROLL TOGETHER LIKE A TIDAL WAVE. THERE ARE NO MANEUVERS OF STRATEGY, NO CAVALRY CHARGES, NO FLIGHTS OF STEEL-TIPPED ARROWS--

--AS *FORTY THOUSAND MEN* FIGHT ON FOOT--- HAND TO HAND, MAN TO MAN, SLAY-ING AND DYING IN RED CHAOS---

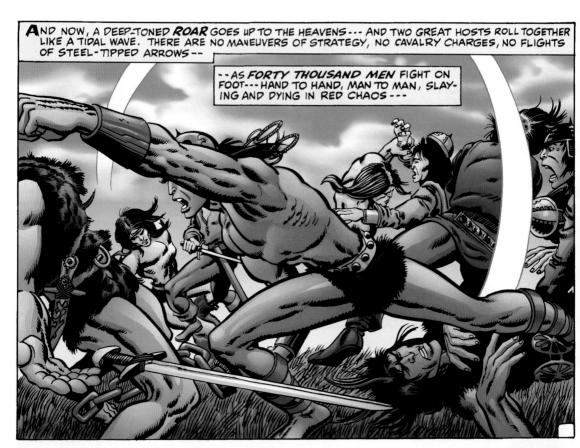

FOR *DUNLANG*, THE DARK PROPHECY OF *EEVIN* IS *FORGOTTEN*-- THOUGH BLOW AFTER BLOW IS WARDED OFF BY MAGIC-FORGED *ARMOR*---

THEN *SUDDENLY*, IN THAT MAD SEA OF BATTLE WHERE WILD FACES COME AND GO LIKE WAVES, THE YOUTH CALLED *CONAN* BEHOLDS A BOLD, BLOND *HYPERBOREAN*-- AND REMEMBERS A *LASH* THAT BIT LIKE AN ANGRY ADDER--

*YOU!!*

I SEE NO GLINT OF *RECOGNITION* IN YOUR EYES. YOU HAVE *FORGOTTEN* ME ---

--BUT I DID NOT FORGET!

CONAN-- THE SAVAGES FIGHT LIKE *MADMEN,* SPURRED ON BY TOMAR'S THREATS OF *DEATH* FOR SHIRKERS.

HASTE FROM THE FRAY TO *MALACHI,* AND BID HIS HORSEMEN *CHARGE,* IN THE NAME OF HEAVEN!

IS THE MAN *BLIND--* OR IS THERE SOME *DARK PURPOSE* IN HIS DELAY?

WE SHALL NEVER *KNOW*-- IF YOU STAND THERE *GAPING* ALL DAY. GO, LAD!

AYE-- BUT ONLY BECAUSE *YOU* ASK IT, FRIEND.

FOR *MYSELF,* I'D STAND AND *FIGHT*-- TILL A *SPEAR* BROUGHT ME DOWN.

MALACHI-- DUNLANG URGES YOU TO *CHARGE..* --OR ELSE THE DAY IS *LOST!*

NAY.

IT IS *NOT* YET TIME.

I WILL CHARGE-- WHEN THE *TIME* COMES.

CONAN SAYS NOTHING, BUT LOOKS INTO THE FURTIVE *EYES* OF MALACHI---AY, PERHAPS INTO HIS VERY *SOUL*-- AND SEES THERE THE BLACK, SPROUTING SEEDS OF--- *TREACHERY.*

DUNLANG! MALACHI SAYS HE WILL CHARGE--WHEN THE *TIME* COMES.

BY THE GODS-- WE ARE *BETRAYED!*

THEN-- THE *DEVIL* TAKE THIS ARMOR! I'LL WEAR IT *NO LONGER!*

LET US *CHARGE*-- LIKE *MEN*--

AND DIEEEE

I KILLED THE BRYTHUNIANS' *LEADER.* NOW THEY ARE *DOOMED.*

IF THEY *ARE,* COWARD--

IT WILL MATTER NOT TO *YOU!*

DUNLANG-- LEAN ON ME, MAN, AND I'LL *CARRY* YOU TO---

NAY-- JUST TELL *EEVIN*-- TELL HER I---

THEN, DUNLANG FALLS LIMP--- AND *CONAN GOES MAD*--!!

NO LONGER DOES HE FIGHT FOR PERSONAL *REVENGE*--BUT FOR A *MEMORY*--A MEMORY WHICH FILLS HIS HEART AND THEWS WITH *FIRE*--

--AND WHICH, FINALLY, FILLS AN *ARMY* WITH THE *WILL TO WIN!*

*BLAST* THAT CHAIN-WIELDING FOOL!

HE'LL YET COST ME MY *KINGDOM* --MY *LIFE!*

BUT, ALL IS NOT YET *LOST*-- IF *BRIAN* DIES AT MY HAND.

AND--YONDER LIE HIS *TENTS!*

*THUS* DO THEY *PASS,* LIKE TWO SHIPS IN THE NIGHT--THE ONE WHO HAS ORDERED *THOUSANDS* TO THEIR DEATHS--

--AND THE OTHER---

--FOR WHOM THE FAST-SETTING SUN SHALL NEVER RISE AGAIN.

THE BATTLE'S *DONE*--AND STILL *MALACHI* STANDS UNMOVING ON THE HILL.

*WAIT* THERE, TRAITOR--JUST A FEW MOMENTS LONGER.

QUICKLY-- *MY HORSE!*

DID YOU *HEAR* ME, YOU SNIVELING--?

WAIT! COME BACK HERE! *DON'T LEAVE ME!*

**COME BACK!**

*HAH!* LOOK AT THAT ONE *WEEP,* FOR SOME FRAIL, FALLEN WARRIOR.

*KORMLADA* KNOWS NO SUCH WEAKNESS-- NO SUCH FOLLY.

THOUGH *TOMAR* BE DEFEATED-- *MALACHI* MAY YET SALVAGE *HONOR* AND *BOOTY* FROM THIS DAY.

AND *KORMLADA* SHALL SALVAGE *MALACHI.*

AH--THERE HE IS-- BUT *WHO*--?

*SPEAK,* BLAST YOU, BARBARIAN-- *SPEAK!*

DON'T JUST DOG MY TRAIL-- LIKE SOME STALKING *WOLF.*

YOU'LL NOT ADD *BRIAN'S* LIFEBLOOD TO YOUR WAR-GOD'S GOBLET.

BORRI IS A *HUNGRY* GOD-- A *THIRSTING* GOD.

HE MUST-- HAVE *BATTLES* TO FEED ON-- OR HE *PERISHES*.

THEN HE HAS SUPPED HIS *LAST*-- WHEN YOU *DIE*--!

PERHAPS YOU SPEAK MORE TRULY THAN YOU *KNOW*, BRYTHUNIAN-- FOR EVEN AS YOU AND TOMAR CARRY YOUR BLOODFEUD INTO THE GLOOMY TWILIGHT, FROM *ABOVE*, A GRIM GREY FORM LOOKS GIGANTICALLY DOWN ---WAITING-- WAITING---

AND *NOW*, SCUM, I'LL---

AiEEEEEEEE!

AAARRHHHH!

TOMAR-- WE--

WE-- *BOTH*--

61

TWO KINGS HAVE DIED THIS DAY--- AND A PITY THEY DIDN'T DIE LONG SINCE.

MANY WOMEN WILL WEEP TONIGHT, ON BOTH SIDES OF THE BORDER.

AND FOR WHAT? FOR THIS!!

THE SUN HAS SUNK NOW, IN A DARK OCEAN OF SCARLET---

GREAT CLOUDS ROLL AND TUMBLE, AND A WIND BLOWS OUT OF THEM---

AND, BORNE ON THAT WIND, ETCHED SHADOWY AGAINST THE CLOUDS---

---RIDE SHAPES WHICH THE YOUNG BARBARIAN HAS SEEN BEFORE---

THE CHOOSERS OF THE SLAIN!

AND WITH THEM --THE GREY MAN!

I SEE IT NOW. HE IS BORRI-- BORRI, THE NORTHERN WAR-GOD--

--SENDING HIS WILD WOMEN TO GATHER LOST SOULS FOR ONE LAST TIME.

FOR, EVEN THE GODS MUST DIE-- WHEN THEIR ALTARS CRUMBLE -- AND THEIR WORSHIPPERS ALL ARE FALLEN.

AND NOW BEGINS THE *CHOOSING* OF THE WORTHY ONES --- AMIDST THE CRIES OF LONG-DEAD *HEROES* WHISTLING IN THE VOID, AND THE SHOUTS OF *FORGOTTEN GODS*.

BUT, IF *SOME* HYPERBOREAN SOULS CRY OUT -- THE TAUT-LIPPED MAIDENS DO NOT SEEM TO *HEAR*.

THEN, IN SOMBER SILENCE, THEY SPUR THEIR WHITE-WINGED MOUNTS *UPWARD* ---

-- SPEEDING THEIR WAY INTO THE *MISTS* FOR THE *FINAL TIME*..

-- AS A BLACK-MANED BARBARIAN SIGHS, AND RECALLS A GOD'S *LAST VOW* --

"SOON YOU SHALL WITNESS THE PASSING OF *KINGS* -- AYE --

"-- AND OF *MORE THAN KINGS!*"

FINIS

63

# CONAN THE BARBARIAN!™

TORCHES FLARE MURKILY IN THE *MAUL* THIS NIGHT... WHERE CERTAIN DENIZENS OF *ARENJUN*, THIEF-CITY OF *ZAMORA*, HOLD THEIR ROARING REVELS.

*STEEL* GLINTS IN THE SHADOWS, WHERE RISES THE SHRILL LAUGHTER OF WOMEN --- AND SNATCHES OF BOISTEROUS *SONG* RUSH OUT THRU WIDE-THROWN DOORS.

WHILE HIGH *ABOVE* THE REST OF THE CITY... ITS JEWELED RIM *GLITTERING* IN THE STARLIGHT --- LOOKS DOWN THE SILENT, SHIMMERING SHAFT WHICH MEN CALL...

# THE TOWER OF THE ELEPHANT!

**STAN LEE** EDITOR • **ROY THOMAS** WRITER • **BARRY SMITH** ARTIST • **SAL BUSCEMA** INKER • **SAM ROSEN** LETTERER

AND, IN ONE OF THE DENS BELOW, *MERRIMENT* THUNDERS TO THE LOW, SMOKE-STAINED ROOF, AS CUTTHROATS AND RASCALS OF ALL NATIONS LISTEN TO THE BAWDY JESTS OF A FAT, GROSS *ROGUE*... A PROFESSIONAL ABDUCTOR COME UP FROM DISTANT *KOTH* TO TEACH WOMAN-STEALING TO ZAMORIANS WHO WERE *BORN* WITH MORE KNOWLEDGE OF THE ART THAN HE COULD EVER HOPE TO ATTAIN...

BY *BEL*, GOD OF *THIEVES*...

*I'LL SHOW* YOU HOW TO STEAL *WENCHES!* I'LL SHOW YOU ALL..!

ADAPTED FROM THE STORY BY *ROBERT E. HOWARD*

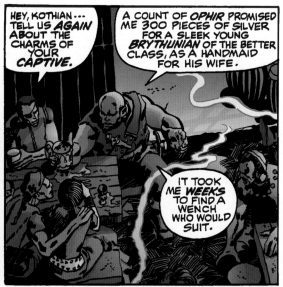

HEY, KOTHIAN... TELL US *AGAIN* ABOUT THE CHARMS OF YOUR *CAPTIVE.*

A COUNT OF *OPHIR* PROMISED ME 300 PIECES OF SILVER FOR A SLEEK YOUNG *BRYTHUNIAN* OF THE BETTER CLASS, AS A HANDMAID FOR HIS WIFE.

IT TOOK ME *WEEKS* TO FIND A WENCH WHO WOULD SUIT.

BUT NOW, I'LL HAVE HER OVER THE ZAMORIAN *BORDER* BY DAWN... WHERE THERE'S A *CARAVAN* WAITING TO RECEIVE HER.

AND IS SHE A *PRETTY* BAGGAGE!

I KNOW LORDS IN *SHEM* WHO WOULD TRADE THE *SECRET OF THE ELEPHANT TOWER* FOR HER!

YOU SPOKE OF THE *ELEPHANT TOWER.* I'VE HEARD *MUCH* OF IT SINCE I CAME TO ARENJUN.

WHAT *IS* ITS SECRET, MAN OF KOTH?

THE *SECRET?* WHY, ER--- ANY *FOOL* KNOWS THAT THE HIGH PRIEST *YARA* DWELLS THERE, WITH THE GREAT JEWEL THAT MEN CALL THE *HEART OF THE ELEPHANT.*

I HAVE *SEEN* THIS TOWER. IT HAS BUT ONE GUARD, AND THE WALLS WOULD BE EASY TO CLIMB.

WHY HAS NOT SOMEONE IN THIS THIEF-CITY *STOLEN* THE JEWEL?

65

LISTEN, BARBARIAN--- FOR SUCH I SEE YOU ARE--- THERE ARE MORE THIEVES IN *ARENJUN* THAN ANYWHERE ELSE IN THE WORLD.

IF MORTAL MAN *COULD* STEAL YARA'S GEM, BE SURE IT WOULD HAVE BEEN FILCHED LONG AGO!

AYE! THERE MAY BE NO *HUMAN* GUARDS IN YARA'S GARDENS.

BUT THERE ARE *SOLDIERS* IN THE LOWER PART OF THE TOWER...

...WHILE THE *JEWEL* IS KEPT SOMEWHERE HIGH *ABOVE*.

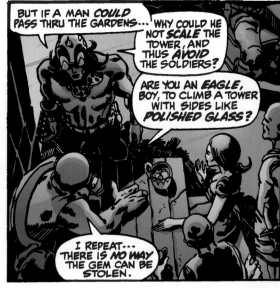

BUT IF A MAN *COULD* PASS THRU THE GARDENS... WHY COULD HE NOT *SCALE* THE TOWER, AND THUS *AVOID* THE SOLDIERS?

ARE YOU AN *EAGLE*, BOY, TO CLIMB A TOWER WITH SIDES LIKE *POLISHED GLASS*?

I REPEAT... THERE IS *NO WAY* THE GEM CAN BE STOLEN.

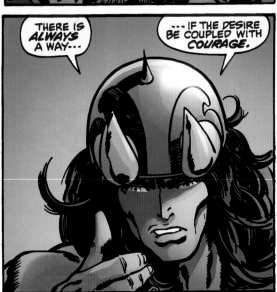

THERE IS *ALWAYS* A WAY...

...IF THE DESIRE BE COUPLED WITH *COURAGE*.

*WHAT?* YOU DARE TELL US OUR BUSINESS, AND THEN INTIMATE THAT WE ARE *COWARDS?*

GET ALONG! GET OUT OF MY *SIGHT!*

FIRST YOU *MOCK* ME--- THEN YOU *LAY HANDS* ON ME.

I'LL STAND FOR *NO MORE!*

WHY, YOU *HEATHEN DOG*--

I'LL HAVE YOUR *HEART* FOR THAT!

SUDDENLY, *STEEL* FLASHES...A SWIRL OF SWORDS WHICH *DIMS* THE FLAME OF THE DEN'S LONE *CANDLE*...

---THEN, PLUNGES THE CHAMBER INTO *DARKNESS* BROKEN ONLY BY A SINGLE AGONIZED *YELL* THAT CUTS THE BLACK NIGHT LIKE A *KNIFE*...!

AT LAST, THE CANDLE IS *RELIGHTED* ---BUT THRONG AND BARBARIAN ALIKE HAVE VANISHED INTO THE SHADOWS, AND---

THE KOTHIAN IS... *DEAD!!*

SOME TIME LATER, A TALL, SILK-CLAD *FORM* DRAWS NIGH THE GLISTENING TOWER---

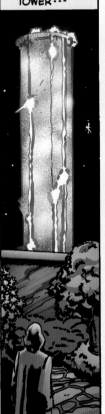

BUT HIS SILENT, STRANGELY SINISTER MOVEMENTS GO NOT *UNNOTICED.*

*OPEN*, SWINE! OPEN THE GATE, I SAY.

WHO *GOES* THERE?

*DOG!* DO YOU NOT KNOW THE VOICE OF *YARA?*

MUST I WORK AN *ENCHANTMENT,* TO PASS THRU MINE OWN *PORTALS?*

A THOUSAND THOUSAND *PARDONS,* GREAT YARA.

I DID NOT KNOW YOU *WALKED ABROAD* THIS NIGHT.

THERE IS *MUCH* YOU DO NOT KNOW, GUARDSMAN.

BEWARE, LEST I *TEACH* YOU IN A WAY YOU *LIKE NOT.*

 SHRUBBERY AND THE NEED FOR STEALTH LIMIT YOUNG CONAN'S *VISION*... LEAVING HIM MERELY A SENSE OF NAMELESS *DREAD* AS THE HIGH PRIEST PASSES SO NEAR TO HIM...

 BUT DOUBTLESS HE WOULD FLEE IN STARK *FEAR*, BACK TOWARD THE WASTES OF HIS BARREN HOMELAND...

 ...IF HE BEHELD THAT, WHERE YARA WALKS, HIS FEET *TOUCH NOT THE GROUND*.

 YET, EVEN SO, THE CIMMERIAN'S HAIR PRICKLES AS HE RECALLS A TALE TOLD HIM BY A DRUNKEN *PAGE* OF THE ZAMORIAN COURT...

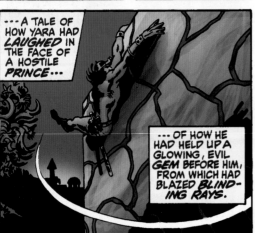 ...A TALE OF HOW YARA HAD *LAUGHED* IN THE FACE OF A HOSTILE *PRINCE*...

...OF HOW HE HAD HELD UP A GLOWING, EVIL *GEM* BEFORE HIM, FROM WHICH HAD BLAZED *BLINDING RAYS*.

 THE PRINCE HAD *SHRUNK DOWN*, SWORE THE PAGE, TO A TINY BLACK *SPIDER*, WHICH HAD SCAMPERED WILDLY ABOUT THE CHAMBER...

 ...UNTIL YARA HAD SET HIS *HEEL* UPON IT!

 WHAT'S *THAT?* A MUFFLED *CRY*...!?

IF I AM *FOUND OUT*, I'LL DIE ATOP A HEAP OF MY *FOES!*

BUT *SILENCE* DRAPES THE *MYSTERIOUS* GARDENS LIKE A *SHROUD*... SO CONAN LOPES TOWARD SOME SHELTERING *SHRUBBERY*...

---ONLY TO *TRIP* OVER A CRUMPLED FORM WHICH LIES *QUITE STILL*...!

WHAT IN THE NAME OF THE *GODS*?

*BY CROM!*

IT'S THE *GUARD* I BEHELD AT THE GATE, MERE MOMENTS AGO.

UNKNOWN *HANDS* HAVE CHOKED OUT HIS LIFE.

*NOW* WHAT ASSAILS MY EARS?

A STEALTHY *FOOTFALL*... AMID THE SHRUBS NEAR THE *WALL!*

*HO,* FELLOW! YOU ARE BULKY AND YOU ARE BRAVE--- BUT AT LEAST YOU ARE *HUMAN.*

*STAND TO,* OR I'LL RUN YOU THRU WITH GOOD *BRYTHUNIAN STEEL.*

YOU ARE NO *SOLDIER,* AS I FEARED.

YOU ARE A *THIEF* LIKE MYSELF... LIKE *TAURUS OF NEMEDIA.*

I'VE HEARD OF YOU. MEN CALL YOU A *PRINCE OF THIEVES.*

AND I'VE *EARNED* THE TITLE A THOUSAND TIMES O'ER--- BUT WHO ARE *YOU?*

I AM *CONAN,* A CIMMERIAN--- AND I CAME SEEK-ING A WAY TO *STEAL* YARA'S *JEWEL*...

...THAT WHICH MEN CALL THE *ELEPHANT'S HEART.*

*HAH!* BY BEL, GOD OF ALL THIEVES!

I HAD THOUGHT THAT ONLY *I* HAD COURAGE ENOUGH TO ATTEMPT *THAT* BIT OF POACH-ING.

AND THOSE *ZAMORIANS* CALL THEMSELVES THIEVES!

I LIKE YOUR *GRIT*, CONAN. WE'LL ATTEMPT THIS ONE *TOGETHER*, IF YOU'VE A MIND TO.

THEN IT WAS *YOU* KILLED THE GUARD?

WHO *ELSE*? I'VE LAID MY PLANS FOR MONTHS--- BUT *YOU*, I THINK, HAVE ACTED ON SUDDEN *IMPULSE*, MY FRIEND.

STILL, I'LL GO AS FAR AS *ANY* MAN.

THEN FOLLOW *ME*.

TELL ME, TAURUS--- WHY DO THEY CALL IT THE TOWER OF THE *ELEPHANT*?

SEARCH *ME*! KNOW YOU WHAT AN ELEPHANT *IS*, LAD?

A MONSTROUS *BEAST*, WITH A TAIL AT BOTH ENDS--- SO A WANDERING *SHEMITE* TOLD ME.

BUT THERE ARE *NO* ELEPHANTS IN ZAMORA.

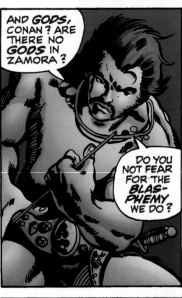

AND *GODS*, CONAN? ARE THERE NO *GODS* IN ZAMORA?

DO YOU NOT FEAR FOR THE *BLAS-PHEMY* WE DO?

WHATEVER GODS *YARA* MAY SACRIFICE TO, THEY ARE NOT *MINE*.

GREAT *CROM* LIVES ON A MOUNTAIN--- AND *LITTLE* HE CARES FOR WHAT MEN DO WITH THEIR TINY LIVES.

CONAN-- *LOOK OUT!*

*LIONS!*

*AYE!* PERHAPS YOU WERE TOLD, THERE ARE NO *HUMAN* GUARDS IN THIS GARDEN.

BUT *FEAR NOT!* WHILE YOU'VE BEEN *TALKING*, I'VE BEEN GETTING *READY* FOR THEM.

THEY BEGIN THEIR CHARGE IN *SILENCE*.

KEEP *BEHIND* ME, LAD--- IF YOU VALUE YOUR *LIFE!*

THEN, THE NEMEDIAN BLOWS POWERFULLY THRU THE *TUBE* WHICH HE HAS FONDLY BRANDISHED---

--- AND A THICK GREEN-YELLOW *CLOUD* DIMS THE FIRE IN SIX GRIM EYES--- *FOREVER*.

THEY *DIED* WITHOUT A WHIMPER.

TAURUS, WHAT *WAS* THAT POWDER?

IT WAS MADE FROM THE MYSTERIOUS *BLACK LOTUS*.

BUT THAT WAS *ALL* I POSSESSED --- I, OR *ANY* MAN EAST OF *KHITAI*.

FROM HERE ON, WE ARE ON OUR *OWN*.

BUT *COME*, IN BEL'S NAME. THE NIGHT GROWS *OLD*.

AH! LUCK THE FIRST *CAST!* I...

*HOLD!*

IT IS CONAN'S SAVAGE *INSTINCTS* WHICH MAKE HIM SUDDENLY *WHEEL*---

--- FOR THE *DEATH* WHICH IS UPON THEM MAKES NO SOUND!

THIS LONE BEAST ESCAPED THE *DEATH OF THE FLOWERS.*

--- BUT HE'LL *NOT* ESCAPE MY *SWORD!*

*ROAR* AS YOU DIE, BLAST YOU! WHY DON'T YOU *ROAR??*

THAT WAS AS *CLOSE* A CALL AS I'VE HAD, IN A LIFE NO-WAYS *TAME.*

ALL THINGS ARE *STRANGE* IN THIS GARDEN.

THE LIONS STRIKE QUIETLY-- AS DO *OTHER* DOOMS.

BUT--THE *SOLDIERS* WITHIN MAY HAVE HEARD THAT SCUFFLE. *COME!*

ON THAT KNOTTED *WISP?* WILL IT BEAR MY WEIGHT?

IT WILL BEAR *THRICE MY OWN,* LAD.

NOW *CLIMB!* MEN SAY THAT YARA HAS LIVED FOR *CENTURIES* BECAUSE OF THE *ELEPHANT'S HEART* GEM---

--- BUT EVEN *HE* CANNOT WAIT *FOREVER* FOR US TO COME STEAL IT.

HE NEED NOT WAIT MUCH *LONGER,* BY CROM.

YET EVEN *CONAN* PAUSES FOR A MOMENT--- DAZZLED BY THE PRECIOUS STONES WHICH DOT THE MIGHTY TOWER ---ALMOST *HYPNOTIZED* BY THEIR THROBBING GLOW---

THERE IS A FABULOUS *FORTUNE* HERE, TAURUS.

IT WILL ALL BE **OURS** -- IF WE FIRST SECURE THE FABLED **HEART**.

AHH -- LUCK IS STILL WITH US. WE'VE REACHED THE TOWER'S RIM **UNSEEN**.

NOW, WE ARE IN THE SERPENT'S OWN **LAIR**.

AYE. THUS, BEFORE WE CUT OFF POSSIBLE **RETREAT** --

GO LOOK OFF THE **OTHER** SIDE -- SEE IF THERE ARE SOLDIERS **THERE**!

ALL RIGHT -- BUT I SEE SCANT **REASON** FOR THIS, TAURUS.

TAURUS --?

HE WENT THRU THAT **DOOR** -- INTO THE **DOME** --

.. WHILE MY **BACK** WAS TURNED.

AARRR

WHAT'S **THAT**? A STRANGLED **CRY** FROM **WITHIN**!

IF THIS IS SOME SORT OF CIVILIZED **TRICK** --

TAURUS!!

WHAT'S **WRONG**, MAN? WHAT'S **INSIDE** THERE --?

DEAD!!

73

AND NOT A **MARK** UPON HIM.

--EXCEPT FOR THOSE TWO TINY **WOUNDS** AT THE BASE OF HIS **NECK**.

WELL, I GUESS I'LL HAVE TO TAKE A LOOK INSIDE --FOR MY-SELF.

--THOUGH IT **SEEMS** EMPTY ENOUGH.

**JEWELS**-- RUBIES, SAPPHIRES, EMERALDS-- STREWN ABOUT IN CARELESS **PROFUSION**. CONAN IS GROWING ALMOST DIZZY AT THE **THOUGHT** OF IT ALL--

--WHEN, ONCE MORE, **DEATH** STRIKES SOUNDLESSLY AT HIM--!

A FLYING **SHADOW** --SOMETHING THAT **SPLASHES** UPON HIS BARE SHOUL-DER AND BURNS LIKE DROPS OF LIQUID **HELLFIRE**--

AND THEN, A SIGHT SUCH AS MEN BEHOLD ONLY IN THEIR DARKEST **NIGHT-MARES**---

A GIGANTIC BLACK **SPIDER**-- ITS FOUR EYES GLEAMING WITH AN EVIL **INTELLIGENCE**, ITS GREAT FANGS DRIPPING **VENOM**!

FOR, YOU SEE, THE UPPER CHAMBER IS GUARDED, AFTER **ALL**.

THEN-- THE MONSTER **LEAPS** AGAIN --

BENEATH THE SHUDDERING IMPACT, THE **SWORD** FLIES FROM CONAN'S HAND--

--AS STRANDS OF FETID **WEBBING** DRAPE ACROSS THE YOUNG BARBARIAN'S WRITHING FORM--

--STRANDS WHICH **GRIP** HIM LIKE THE COILS OF THE FABLED **PYTHON.**

SO, YOU HAIRY DEVIL --YOU **GUARD** THIS BOOTY, DO YOU?

THEN, ONE **FINAL** LUNGE--

WELL THEN-- YOU CAN **HAVE** IT!

DEAD! AND I WONDER WHO **YOU** WERE, MONSTER--

--BEFORE YARA SET HIS **SPIDER-SPELL** ON YOU.

HUHNN-- I DIDN'T NOTICE **THIS** DOOR BEFORE.

MIGHT AS WELL FIND OUT WHERE IT **LEADS.**

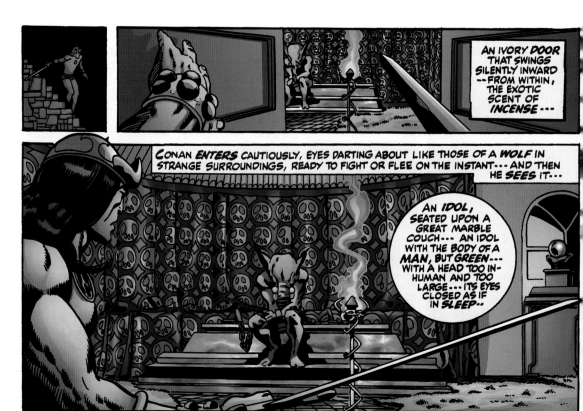

AN IVORY *DOOR* THAT SWINGS SILENTLY INWARD --FROM WITHIN, THE EXOTIC SCENT OF *INCENSE* ---

CONAN *ENTERS* CAUTIOUSLY, EYES DARTING ABOUT LIKE THOSE OF A *WOLF* IN STRANGE SURROUNDINGS, READY TO FIGHT OR FLEE ON THE INSTANT --- AND THEN HE *SEES* IT ---

AN *IDOL*, SEATED UPON A GREAT MARBLE COUCH --- AN IDOL WITH THE BODY OF A *MAN*, BUT *GREEN* --- WITH A HEAD TOO IN-HUMAN AND TOO LARGE --- ITS EYES CLOSED AS IF IN *SLEEP* --

AND THEN ---

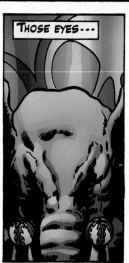

THOSE EYES ---

--OPEN!

PARALYZED WITH TERROR-- HELD FAST BY FEAR-- THE CIMMERIAN *FREEZES* IN HIS TRACKS. THIS IS NO IDOL, BUT A *LIVING THING* --

--AND HE IS *TRAPPED* WITHIN ITS CHAMBER!

JUST THEN, THE *TRUNK* OF THE HORROR IS LIFTED-- QUESTS ABOUT, AS TOPAZ EYES STARE *UNSEEING*-- AND THE CREATURE *SPEAKS* IN A STAMMERING VOICE, THRU JAWS NEVER MEANT FOR *HUMAN SPEECH* ...

WHO IS *HERE* ? HAVE YOU COME TO TORMENT ME *AGAIN*, YARA?

OH, YAG-KOSHA-- IS THERE NEVER TO BE AN END TO YOUR AGONY?

AS *TEARS* ROLL FROM SIGHTLESS EYES, CONAN'S GAZE FALLS UPON THE *CHAINS* WHICH HOLD THE MONSTER--AND SUDDENLY HIS FEAR AND REVULSION ARE REPLACED BY A DEEPLY FELT *PITY*---

I AM *NOT* YARA.

I AM-- ONLY A *THIEF.*

I WILL NOT *HARM* YOU.

COME *NEAR*--THAT YAG-KOSHA MAY *TOUCH* YOU.

YOU ARE NOT OF YARA'S RACE OF DEVILS.

THE CLEAN, LEAN FIERCENESS OF THE WASTE-LANDS MARKS YOU.

YES, FEEL MY TRUNK--FOR I AM NEITHER GOD NOR DEMON--BUT FLESH AND BONE LIKE YOURSELF.

BUT--THERE IS *BLOOD* ON YOUR FINGERS.

A *SPIDER* IN THE CHAMBER ABOVE--

--AND A *LION* IN THE GARDEN.

YOU HAVE SLAIN A *MAN,* TOO, THIS NIGHT--AND THERE IS *HUMAN DEATH* IN THE TOWER ABOVE.

I FEEL! I KNOW!

LISTEN, O MAN! I AM FOUL AND MON-STROUS TO YOU, I KNOW--BUT YOU WOULD SEEM AS STRANGE TO ME, COULD I BUT SEE YOU.

FOR, THERE ARE MANY WORLDS BESIDES THIS EARTH--AND LIFE TAKES MANY SHAPES...

"LONG AND LONG AGO, I CAME TO THIS PLANET WITH OTHERS OF MY WORLD -- FROM THE GREEN PLANET YAG, ON THE OUTER FRINGES OF THE UNIVERSE---

"OUR MIGHTY WINGS SWEPT US THRU SPACE FAR FASTER THAN LIGHT ITSELF---

"BUT WHEN WE CAME TO THIS WORLD, OUR WINGS FELL FROM OUR SHOULDERS--

"-- SO THAT WE COULD NEVER LEAVE IT.

"WE FOUGHT THE STRANGE AND TERRIBLE BEASTS WHICH THEN WALKED THE EARTH -- AND WE MADE THE DIM JUNGLES OF THE EAST OUR ABODE ---

"DWELLING THUS APART, WE WATCHED MAN GROW FROM THE APE -- TO BUILD THE SHINING CITIES OF VALUSIA AND HER SISTER KINGDOMS ---

"--AND WE SAW THE OCEANS RISE ONE DAY, TO DRINK ATLANTIS AND ALL THE GREAT-TOWERED CITIES OF CIVILIZATION."

" ALL THIS WE SAW -- AND ONE BY ONE WE DIED -- FOR, WE ARE NOT IMMORTAL, THOUGH OUR LIVES ARE AS THE LIVES OF THE STARS THEM-SELVES---

"AT LAST I ALONE WAS LEFT -- WOR-SHIPPED AS A GOD IN JUNGLE-LOST KHITAI---

"THEN CAME YARA -- WELL VERSED IN DARK ARTS HANDED DOWN FROM DAYS OF YORE ---

" FIRST HE SAT AT MY FEET AND LEARNED WISDOM -- BUT ONE DAY, HE TURNED MY OWN POWER UPON ME -- AND ENSLAVED ME.

"HE PENT ME IN THIS TOWER WHICH AT HIS COMMAND I BUILT FOR HIM IN A SINGLE NIGHT.

" BY FIRE AND RACK HE MASTERED ME --- AND SO FOR THREE HUNDRED YEARS I HAVE DONE HIS FOUL BIDDING--

"YET NOT ALL MY ANCIENT SECRETS HAS HE WRESTED FROM ME -- AND MY LAST GIFT SHALL BE THE SORCERY OF THE BLOOD AND THE JEWEL!"

As the monster finishes his tale, a strange aching **sadness** comes over **Conan** -- and he senses, somehow, that he is in the presence of some **cosmic tragedy** -- and he shrinks with shame, as if the guilt of a whole **race** were laid upon him ---

But now, the **end** of my time draws near -- and **you** are the hand of **fate**.

I beg of you -- look upon the gem on yonder altar.

And Conan **looks** -- and he knows that he gazes upon -- **the heart of the elephant.**

Take your sword, O man -- and drive it into my breast!

Then, go you down to the ebony chamber where Yara dreams --- and lay the gem before him -- and say --

"Yag-Kosha gives you a last **gift** -- and a last **enchantment!**"

Then **flee** the tower -- quickly.

Well? Strike, O man -- if you feel pity for Yag-Kosha --

**STRIKE!**

The Brythunian blade is **heavy** in Conan's great hand -- then, without a word, the young barbarian sets his teeth -- and **drives it deep** --!

FARE YOU **WELL**, YAG-KOSHA!

I NEVER KILLED **ANOTHER** FOE WITH SO **UN-WILLING** A THRUST.

HOLD! NOW-- THE BLAZING **JEWEL**--

IT TURNS-- THE COLOR OF **BLOOD**!

THEN-- I MUST FULFILL THE **FINAL WISH**-- OF YAG-KOSHA.

**SILENT**, HE LIES IN HIS JET-BLACK CHAMBER-- THE **HIGH PRIEST** AND **SORCERER**-- HIS EYES DILATED WITH THE FUMES OF THE YELLOW LOTUS-- **FAR-STARING**, AS IF FIXED ON GULFS AND NIGHTED ABYSSES BEYOND HUMAN KEN---

YARA! AWAKEN!

**DOG!**

WHO **ARE** YOU? WHAT DO YOU WANT **HERE**??

WELL, CUR? *SPEAK UP,* BEFORE I..

HE WHO *SENT* THIS GEM BADE ME SAY...

"*YAG-KOSHA* GIVES A LAST *GIFT* -- AND A LAST EN-CHANTMENT!"

*NO!* NO -- IT CANNOT BE!

HE *CANNOT* ESCAPE ME THUS. I AM HIS MASTER-- *HIS MASTER!*

LIKE A MAN IN A *DREAM,* YARA GRIPS THE MURKY JEWEL IN HIS HANDS-- STARING INTO ITS SHADOWED *DEPTHS* AS IF THEY WOULD DRAW THE SHUDDERING *SOUL* FROM HIS BODY---

AND THEN-- AS CONAN LOOKS ON IN GROWING *HORROR*---

-- HE REALIZES THAT THE HIGH PRIEST IS *SHRINKING* IN STATURE-- GROWING SMALLER, *SMALLER* BEFORE HIS VERY EYES---

NOW, THE SCARLET GEM *TOWERS* ABOVE YARA LIKE A *HILL* ---

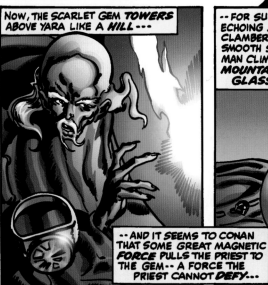

-- AND IT SEEMS TO CONAN THAT SOME GREAT MAGNETIC *FORCE* PULLS THE PRIEST TO THE GEM-- A FORCE THE PRIEST CANNOT *DEFY*---

-- FOR SUDDENLY, WITH A FAINTLY ECHOING *SCREAM,* YARA CLAMBERS IMPOSSIBLY UP ITS SMOOTH SURFACE-- LIKE A MAN CLIMBING A *MOUNTAIN OF GLASS* --

..ONLY TO *SINK* INTO THE VERY CENTER OF THE JEWEL--

-- AS A MAN SINKS INTO A VAST AND BECKONING *SEA.*

AND NOW, CONAN SEES YARA IN THE CRIMSON *HEART* OF THE JEWEL-- AS *INTO* THAT HEART SWOOPS A SHINING, WINGED *FIGURE*--

YAG-KOSHA!

NO LONGER *MAIMED*-- NO LONGER *BLIND!*

THROWING UP HIS ARMS, YARA FLEES AS A *MADMAN* FLEES--

--AND ON HIS HEELS COMES THE *AVENGER!*

NEXT, AS IF FROM OVER A VAST *DISTANCE*, CONAN HEARS--

"*THE LIFE OF MAN IS NOT THE LIFE OF YAG-KOSHA --NOR IS HUMAN DEATH, HIS DEATH!*"

THEN, LIKE THE BURSTING OF A BUBBLE, THE THROBBING JEWEL *VANISHES*-- IN A RAINBOW FLARING OF IRRIDESCENT *GLEAMS*--

--AND CONAN'S GREAT HANDS ARE EMPTY.. *BARE* --

--AS **BARE,** CONAN SOMEHOW KNOWS, AS THAT **MARBLE COUCH** IN THE CHAMBER ABOVE MUST BE.

THEN, THE TOWER BEGINS TO **SHAKE**--

CONAN TURNS --AND **FLEES** DOWN-WARD--

FOR, THE **SOLDIERS** BELOW ARE FOREVER STILLED BY **MAGIC**-- AND A SILVER **DOOR** STANDS OPEN, FRAMED IN THE WHITENESS OF DAWN---

**O**UT INTO THE WAVING GREEN **GARDENS** RUNS THE CIMMERIAN--- AND, AS THE MORNING WIND BLOWS UPON HIM, HE **STARTS** LIKE A MAN WAKING FROM A NIGHTMARE.

AND, AS HE LOOKS BACK, HE SEES THE GLEAMING TOWER **SWAY** AMIDST THE CRIMSON DAWN-- ITS JEWEL-CRUSTED RIM **SPARKLING** IN THE GROWING LIGHT---

--AS THE **TOWER OF THE ELEPHANT** CRASHES INTO SHINING SHARDS!

*Finis.*

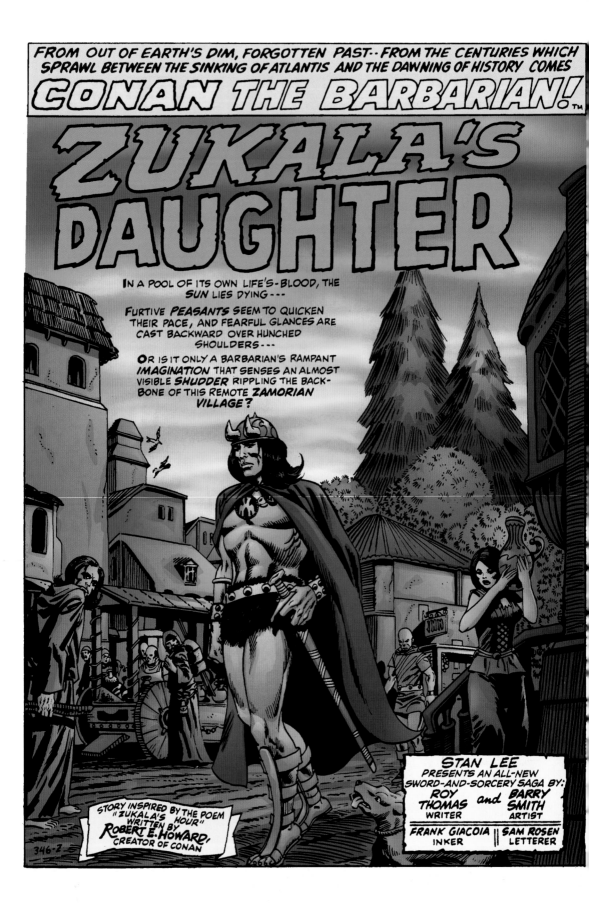

FROM OUT OF EARTH'S DIM, FORGOTTEN PAST--FROM THE CENTURIES WHICH SPRAWL BETWEEN THE SINKING OF ATLANTIS AND THE DAWNING OF HISTORY COMES

# CONAN THE BARBARIAN!™

## ZUKALA'S DAUGHTER

IN A POOL OF ITS OWN LIFE'S-BLOOD, THE SUN LIES DYING---

FURTIVE PEASANTS SEEM TO QUICKEN THEIR PACE, AND FEARFUL GLANCES ARE CAST BACKWARD OVER HUNCHED SHOULDERS---

OR IS IT ONLY A BARBARIAN'S RAMPANT IMAGINATION THAT SENSES AN ALMOST VISIBLE SHUDDER RIPPLING THE BACKBONE OF THIS REMOTE ZAMORIAN VILLAGE?

STORY INSPIRED BY THE POEM "ZUKALA'S HOUR" WRITTEN BY ROBERT E. HOWARD, CREATOR OF CONAN

346-2

STAN LEE PRESENTS AN ALL-NEW SWORD-AND-SORCERY SAGA BY:
ROY THOMAS WRITER and BARRY SMITH ARTIST
FRANK GIACOIA INKER || SAM ROSEN LETTERER

ON YOUR WAY TO *SHADIZAR THE WICKED,* ARE YE? VISITED THE PLACE ONCE *MYSELF,* WHEN I WERE YOUNGER.

YE'LL DO WELL WITH THE *LADIES* THERE, IF YE'LL BUY THIS *SWORD--* A *STEAL* AT SEVEN DRAKIS.

A STEAL FOR *YOU,* MAYBE.

BECAUSE IT'S *YOU,* LAD, I'LL MAKE IT *SIX···*

I'VE ONLY GOT *ONE,* SO-- *BY CROM!* HOW QUICKLY THE SKY GROWS *BLACK!*

IT IS TIME. *IT IS TIME!*

*FLEE,* MY BROTHERS-- LOCK YOUR DOORS, AND BAR YOUR WINDOWS!

*AIEEE!* IN MY *GREED,* I FORGOT.

I MEANT TO CLOSE MY SHOP *EARLY* THIS DAY OF DAYS-- BUT I *FORGOT!*

FORGOT *WHAT,* MAN? WHY IS EVERYONE RUNNING LIKE STARTLED TOADS?

*ANSWER* ME, SMITHY, OR I'LL ---

*NO--* PLEASE-- I'LL *TELL* YE---

BUT-- I DARE NOT BE *LONG* ABOUT IT.

IT'S OUR *TAXES,* Y'SEE.

FORTY PIECES OF *GOLD--* DUE THIS SAME DAY, EACH AND EVERY *YEAR.*

WE HAVEN'T *PAID* THEM-- AND NOW THE *MASTER'LL* BE SENDING SOMEONE TO-- *COLLECT* 'EM.

*FOOL!* DO YOU THINK THE DRUNKEN KING OF ZAMORA EVEN *REMEMBERS* THIS STINKING HOLE?

I-- DID NOT SPEAK OF THE *KING. LOOK,* BARBARIAN --*LOOK!*

MY EYES MAKE *SPORT* WITH ME.

IS THAT A *CAT'S HEAD* I SEE--- FORMING OUT OF THE VERY *MIST?*

*MORE* THAN A CAT, STRANGER-- FAR, *FAR* MORE.

IT IS *SHE-- SHE!*

SHE, SMITH? WHO DO YOU--?

MORRIGAN, MACHA, AND NEMAIN!!

THIS STRONGEST OF *OATHS* TORN FROM HIS LIPS, THE YOUNG CIMMERIAN STANDS SUDDENLY *FROZEN* -- SENSING THAT HE IS IN THE PRESENCE OF A THING *NOT OF THIS WORLD* ---

-- A SENSATION *SHATTERED* THE NEXT INSTANT, AS KNIFE-EDGED *TALONS* SPLINTER A FLIMSY WOODEN CART ---

HAH! THAT'S NO *GHOST-BEAST*, FELLOW --

--BUT A CREATURE AS REAL AS THE *LION* I SLEW IN THE GARDENS OF *YARA*.

I NEVER *DID* LIKE THE IDEA OF FLEEING LIKE A HARE-- NOT WHILE I'VE GOT A *SWORD-HILT* IN MY FIST.

BESIDES, *THERE'S* TWO WHO DIDN'T RUN *FAST* ENOUGH --

AND ONE OF THEM IS A *PRETTY* PACKAGE, TO *BOOT!*

86

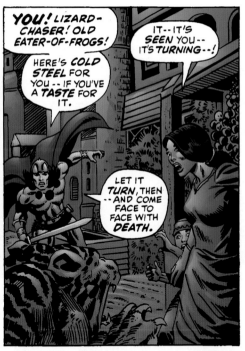

**YOU!** LIZARD-CHASER! OLD EATER-OF-FROGS!

HERE'S **COLD STEEL** FOR YOU -- IF YOU'VE A **TASTE** FOR IT.

IT--IT'S **SEEN** YOU -- IT'S **TURNING**--!

LET IT **TURN**, THEN --AND COME FACE TO FACE WITH **DEATH**.

BUT, ON THE INSTANT, IT IS THE **BARBARIAN** WHO GLIMPSES THE GRINNING SKULL OF DOOM--AS **STRIPED LIGHTNING** CRACKLES --

--AND MAN-FORGED **METAL** GIVES WAY LIKE A BLADE OF BRITTLE **GLASS!**

**MIGHTY** IS THE YOUTH CALLED **CONAN** -- LIKE A HEADSTRONG YOUNG BULL OF THE MARSHLANDS---

---YET THE SPRINGING **TIGRESS** HURLS HIM FROM HIS FEET AS IF HE WERE, INSTEAD, SOME TREMBLING **CALF**--

--AS VISE-LIKE **JAWS** CLAMP DOWN WITH FORCE ENOUGH TO REND FLESH FROM GLEAMING BONE -- IF THEY WOULD BUT **MOVE!**

**CROM'S DEVILS!**

YOU **ARE** A DEMON-THING, AFTER **ALL**.

THEN -- WHY DON'T YOU **STRIKE**--AND HAVE **DONE** WITH IT?

IS IT SOME FEAR-SPAWNED *FANTASY* THAT HAPPENS NEXT-- SOME FLEETING *PHANTOM* OF THE MIND AND SENSES---

--THAT NOW MAKES CONAN THINK HE HEARS A *VOICE*--

--A WHISPER FROM THE NETHER SIDE OF THE *UNIVERSE*, THAT SEEMS TO SAY: "*I SHALL NOT HARM YOU. NOT NOW. NOT EVER.*"

THEN, LIKE A SOUNDLESS *SPECTRE*--

HOLD! COME *BACK*--!

COME--- BACK.

*WHAT?* YOU'RE A *BRAVE* ONE-- BUT ARE YE *DAFT*, AS WELL?

IF SHE RETURNS --SHE'LL BE THIRSTING FOR *ALL* OUR BLOODS.

MAYBE HE'S IN *LEAGUE* WITH HER. WHY ELSE DIDN'T SHE *KILL* HIM WHEN SHE HAD A CHANCE?

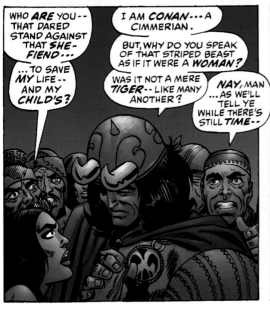

WHO *ARE* YOU-- THAT DARED STAND AGAINST THAT *SHE-FIEND*---

...TO SAVE *MY* LIFE-- AND MY *CHILD'S*?

I AM *CONAN*---A CIMMERIAN.

BUT, WHY DO YOU SPEAK OF THAT STRIPED BEAST AS IF IT WERE A *WOMAN*?

WAS IT NOT A MERE *TIGER*-- LIKE MANY ANOTHER?

*NAY*, MAN ...AS WE'LL TELL YE WHILE THERE'S STILL *TIME*--

"FOR, WE'LL DOUBTLESS *PAY* FOR THIS RESPITE ANYWAY-- AND *SOONER* THAN WE'D LIKE!"

"A BEAST LIKE ANY OTHER, DID YE SAY? YE'D KNOW YOUR FOLLY, OUTLANDER, IF YE COULD GAZE UPON THAT RIBBONED FORM NOW...

"Y'SEE, THERE'S THOSE WHO'VE HIDDEN OUT IN THE SHADOW OF THE MOON...

"...AND VOW THEY'VE SEEN HER SHED HER FELINE SPELL--- TO WALK AS A WOMAN ONCE MORE.

"YET, THERE'S OTHERS SAY WE SHOULD FEEL NO SCORN FOR ZEPHRA-- DAUGHTER OF ZUKALA--

"FOR SHE WAS BORN WHEN THE WIND WAS OUT OF THE NORTH--- AND WHEN THE GREY LIGHT LIFTED FOR MORN-- THAT TIME WHICH IS CALLED-- ZUKALA'S HOUR!

"SUCH ONES, THEY SAY, ARE CURSED WITH SECOND SIGHT--- THE POWER TO LIFT THE VEIL THAT HIDES THE FUTURE--

"AND CAN IT BE A KINDNESS TO FORESEE-- THE HOUR OF YOUR OWN DEATH?"

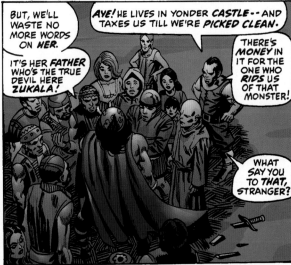

BUT, WE'LL WASTE NO MORE WORDS ON HER.

IT'S HER FATHER WHO'S THE TRUE DEVIL HERE ZUKALA!

AYE! HE LIVES IN YONDER CASTLE-- AND TAXES US TILL WE'RE PICKED CLEAN.

THERE'S MONEY IN IT FOR THE ONE WHO RIDS US OF THAT MONSTER!

WHAT SAY YOU TO THAT, STRANGER?

I SAY-- I'LL HEAR MORE ABOUT THIS ZUKALA---

--OVER A FLAGON OF FRESH-POURED WINE.

89

OF COURSE, OF **COURSE**! BUT FIRST, LET US TEND TO YOUR **WOUNDS**--

THEY'RE ONLY **SCRATCHES**. TELL ME OF **ZUKALA**, AND OF HIS TIGRESS **DAUGHTER**.

IT'S SAID THEY'RE **AGELESS**-- THAT TIME CAN NEVER TOUCH THEM.

AND **TRUE** IT IS-- FOR ONCE I BEHELD THE GIRL, DANCING 'NEATH THE STARS, WHEN **SHE** WAS YOUNG, AND **I** WAS YOUNG.

NOW SHE IS **STILL** YOUNG-- WHILE I GROW OLD AND **WITHERED**.

WHERE'S THE FAIRNESS IN THAT? **DEATH** TO THEM, SAYS I--

"--DEATH TO THEM **BOTH**!"

FATHER--?

**ZEPHRA**, MY DARLING.

HAVE MY BELOVED SUBJECTS SENT THEIR JUST **TRIBUTE** AT LAST?

**NO**, MY FATHER---

THE UN-GRATEFUL **SWINE**!

THEY--SET FORTH **NO GOLD** FOR ME--- THEY--

BUT, WHY SO **PALE**, MY PET-- LIKE SOME THIN-BLOODED **MORTAL**?

I--I DO NOT **KNOW**, SIRE. I---

90

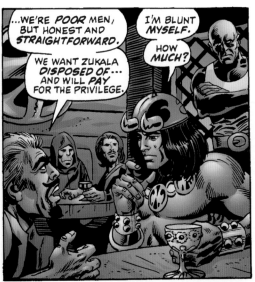

...WE'RE *POOR* MEN, BUT HONEST AND *STRAIGHTFORWARD.*

WE WANT ZUKALA *DISPOSED OF* --- AND WILL *PAY* FOR THE PRIVILEGE.

I'M *BLUNT* MYSELF.

HOW *MUCH?*

FORTY PIECES OF GOLD -- THE SAME PRICE THAT DEVIL-WIZARD WOULD EXACT FROM *US* -- TO BE PAID ONE *LAST* YEAR ---

*ALMOST* ENOUGH --- -- BUT NOT *QUITE.*

-- BUT THIS TIME, TO *YOU.*

WHAT *ELSE* WOULD YOU HAVE? WE'RE NOT *RICH BARONS,* LIKE THOSE YOU DOUBTLESS HOPE TO ROB IN *SHADIZAR.*

WOULD YOU LEAVE US *NO-THING?*

I WANT NO MORE *MONEY.* OLD MAN -- JUST A CERTAIN *WEAPON* --

THE DRAGON-HILT *BLADE* WHICH THE SWORDSMITH TRIED TO SELL ME.

*DONE.* AND A *SMALL* PRICE TO PAY, FOR FREEDOM FROM THAT SORCEROUS *TYRANT!*

THEN, I'LL *GET* IT --- AND BE ON MY *WAY.*

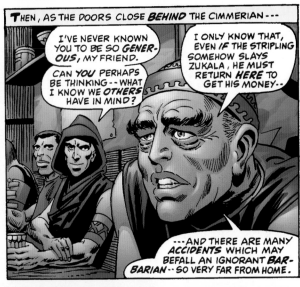

*THEN,* AS THE DOORS CLOSE *BEHIND* THE CIMMERIAN ---

I'VE NEVER KNOWN YOU TO BE SO *GENER-OUS,* MY FRIEND.

CAN *YOU* PERHAPS BE THINKING -- WHAT I KNOW WE *OTHERS* HAVE IN MIND?

I ONLY KNOW THAT, EVEN *IF* THE STRIPLING SOMEHOW SLAYS ZUKALA, HE MUST RETURN *HERE* TO GET HIS MONEY --

--- AND THERE ARE MANY *ACCIDENTS* WHICH MAY BEFALL AN IGNORANT *BAR-BARIAN* -- SO VERY FAR FROM HOME.

High in his dim, ghost-haunted Tower Zukala sits alone ---

Like a spider, spinning his webs of *power* Upon his moon-pale throne ---

All through the long, star-spectral **night**
The tower knows no tread···

···Save for, sometimes, the eerie, light
Swift footfalls of the **dead**···

He **does not sleep** and his eyes are deep
As the seas of Falgarai···

And he moves
his sceptre
but to sweep
The dim **stars**
out of the sky.

And when the wind is out of the **east**
And the bent moon's silver gleam
Makes pale the stars like **ghosts** at feast···

···Zukala sits a-dream···!

BEFORE ZAMORA WAS, **ACHERON** WAS-- THAT MOST EVIL OF EMPIRES -- AND **PYTHON**, ITS PURPLE-TOWERED CITY--

--NOW **DEAD** THESE THREE THOUSAND YEARS, TRAMPLED 'NEATH BARBARIAN HEELS--!

BEFORE ACHERON WAS, **ATLANTIS** WAS-- AND THE MAN-LEGEND **KULL**, WHO ROSE TO SIT THE TOPAZ THRONE--!

AND BEFORE ATLANTIS WAS --**I WAS!**

--THE **CALL** OF **ZUKALA!**

COME, THUS, IN **MY NAME**-- AT **MY** CALL--

I HAVE JOURNEYED, O WIZARD, FROM OUT THE **LOST LAND**-- IN ANSWER TO THY SUMMONS.

WHAT **WILT** THOU OF THE DEMON **JAGGTA-NOGA**-- FOR, THAT MUST HE **DO!**

**YOU** MUST ACCOMPLISH -- WHAT MY DAUGHTER COULD **NOT.**

THE **VILLAGERS** BEYOND ARE WITHHOLDING FROM ME MY PROPER **TRIBUTE**-- MINE BY RIGHT OF **POWER.**

I WANT THEM **STRIPPED** OF THAT TRIBUTE--

-- OR I WANT THEM **DEAD!**

NOW **GO**--- AND DO YOU MY **BIDDING**!

THE PEASANTS' GOLD MEANS **LITTLE** TO ME -- BUT IT REMINDS THE FOOLS JUST WHO IS **MASTER** --AND WHO IS **SLAVE**.

I **GO**--AND I **OBEY**, O WIZARD.

**NOW**, WANDERER-- YOU SHALL TELL ME **WHY** YOU HAVE --

KEEP YOUR MOUTH **SHUT**, UNTIL--- AHHH-- HIS STEPS **RECEDE** DOWN THE CORRIDOR.

=EMMFFF!=

YOU CAN ONLY BE **ZEPHRA**-- DAUGHTER OF THE ONE CALLED **ZUKALA**.

IS IT TRUE YOU CAN SEE THE **FUTURE** --AND THAT YOU CAN TURN YOURSELF INTO-- A **WILD BEAST**?

I'VE SEEN **STRANGE THINGS** IN MY DAY, BUT **THAT**--

--IS HARD TO **BELIEVE**, CONAN?

**BELIEVE**, ALL THE **SAME**-- FOR HOW ELSE WOULD I **KNOW** YOUR **NAME**?

BELIEVE **THIS** ALSO-- THAT, IN THE MOMENT WE **CLASHED**-- AND AGAIN, WHEN I **FAINTED**, CHILD-LIKE, IN MY FATHER'S ARMS--

I KNEW YOU WERE THE MAN I MUST **LOVE**-- THE MAN WHO SHALL WATCH THE **AGES** FLOW, AT MY **SIDE**.

**WHAT**? WHOA-- SLOW DOWN, GIRL-- THIS ALL GOES **TOO FAST** FOR ME.

**LIFE** GOES TOO FAST, CONAN-- FOR I HAVE LOOKED INTO OUR **FUTURES**, YOURS AND MINE--

AND I HAVE DIMLY SEEN YOU STANDING OVER MY **BODY**--

--A GLEAMING **AXE** IN YOUR GREAT HANDS.

BUT-- HOLD ME, MY LOVE --**HOLD ME**!

FOR, THAT MOMENT MAY BE A **YEAR** AWAY-- OR A **CENTURY**--

OR IT MAY **NEVER** HAPPEN, MY DAUGHTER!

--NOT IF I *SLAY* THIS BASE INTERLOPER-- AND LET *JAGGTA-NOGA* DRAG HIS SOUL BACK TO THE *LOST LAND!*

NO, FATHER-- *NO!*

*CROM'S DEVILS!* DO DOORS MEAN *NOTHING* IN THIS PLACE?

BUT, NO MATTER -- FOR, YOU'RE SOLID ENOUGH *NOW.*

MAKE READY TO *PAY,* WIZARD, FOR THE *SINS* OF ALL THE YEARS YOU HAVE LIVED.

*INSOLENT PUP!* USE THAT WEAPON TO STICK *PIGS--*

-- NOT TO THREATEN THE LIKES OF *ZUKALA!*

BY ANY RIGHTS, YOUNG CONAN NOW SHOULD *DIE*--- BY ANY RIGHTS THE *BURST* WHICH FLASHES LIKE LIGHTNING SHOULD REDUCE HIM TO WHIMPERING *ATOMS*---

*BUT,* THE CIMMERIAN MOVES MORE *SWIFTLY* THAN ANY TIMID *ZAMORIAN--* HE *EVADES* THE SPARK THAT WOULD HAVE ENGULFED HIM---

*AND* THEN, LIKE A WOLF AT BAY, HE *STRIKES*--!

WHAT *MADNESS* IS THIS? I HIT HIM *FULL FORCE* -- AND MERELY *STAGGERED* HIM!?

WELL, ONE *MORE* BLOW, AND SURELY--

*NO,* CONAN-- LET HIM *GO*--- *PLEASE*..

*MY MASK! MY MASK*--!

95

96

MAYBE I *WOULD*--IF YOUR *AIM* WERE THE *EQUAL* OF YOUR *MAGIC.*

BUT NOW, MY *NEXT* BLOW WILL SPLIT YOUR SKULL AS EASILY AS I SPLINTERED THAT *ALTAR.*

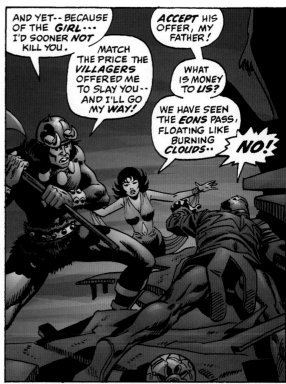

AND YET-- BECAUSE OF THE *GIRL*... I'D SOONER *NOT* KILL YOU.

*MATCH* THE PRICE THE *VILLAGERS* OFFERED ME TO SLAY YOU-- AND I'LL GO MY *WAY!*

*ACCEPT* HIS OFFER, MY *FATHER!*

WHAT IS MONEY TO *US?*

WE HAVE SEEN THE *EONS* PASS, FLOATING LIKE BURNING *CLOUDS...*

*NO!*

IT IS TRUE-- THAT I *UNDERESTIMATED* THE BARBARIAN--- FOR IT HAS BEEN *LONG* SINCE ANY DARED *DEFY* ME.

BUT NOW-- THE THIRST FOR *TRIUMPH* MINGLES WITH THE BLOOD IN MY THROAT-- AND IT MUST BE *SATISFIED!*

*ZEPHRA!* BECOME ONCE MORE THE RAGING *BEAST* YOU WERE -- AND REND THE FOOL *LIMB* FROM *LIMB!*

THUS DO *I* COMMAND --I, *ZUKALA*-- YOUR *FATHER!*

AND-- BECAUSE IT IS MY *FATHER* WHO COMMANDS ME---

CAN I-- *REFUSE* THE CALL--?

THE **TIGRESS!**

THEN-- THE VILLAGERS SPOKE THE **TRUTH.**

THE **LAST** TRUTH THAT YOU SHALL EVER **KNOW.**

SLAY HIM MY DAUGHTER! SLAY HIM!

BUT **AGAIN,** AS IF IN A DREAM, COMES THAT WORLD-DISTANT WHISPER: "NO, FATHER! I SHALL **NOT** HARM HIM. NOT **NOW.** NOT **EVER.**"

THEN-- YOU HAVE **DOOMED** YOUR SIRE-- BENEATH THIS SAVAGE'S **AXE!**

NOT IF THOU DOST NOT **WISH** TO DIE, O WIZARD!

WHAT **VOICE** IS THAT--- WHICH ECHOES AS IF FROM BEYOND THE **GRAVE?**

FROM BEYOND **YOUR** GRAVE AT LEAST, FOOL.

**TURN,** BARBARIAN-- AND SEE THE FACE AND FORM OF **FEAR INCARNATE!**

**CROM!**

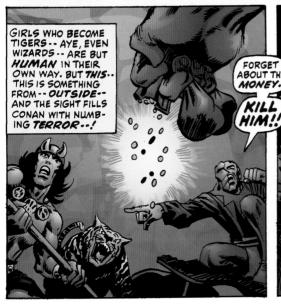

GIRLS WHO BECOME TIGERS-- AYE, EVEN **WIZARDS**-- ARE BUT **HUMAN** IN THEIR OWN WAY. BUT **THIS**-- THIS IS SOMETHING FROM-- **OUTSIDE**-- AND THE SIGHT FILLS CONAN WITH NUMBING **TERROR**--!

FORGET ABOUT THE **MONEY.**

**KILL HIM!!**

AS YOU **DESIRE,** O WIZARD. BUT-- WHAT **CREATURE** IS THIS-- WHICH LEAPS HEADLONG TO ITS OWN **DEATH?**

ZEPHRA-- **NO!**

RRRR RRRR

CAUGHT *OFF GUARD* BY THIS SHE-BEAST, AS MAGICAL AS HIMSELF, THE HELL-FIEND *FALLS* WITH THUNDEROUS IMPACT--

--ONLY TO *RISE AGAIN!*

KILL HER, THING OF THE NETHER DEPTHS--

AND THEN *TURN*--TURN UPON THE *BARBARIAN!*

WHAT ARE YOU *SAYING*, MAN?

WOULD YOU DOOM YOUR OWN *DAUGH-TER*--JUST BECAUSE SHE WOULD NOT DESTROY *ME?*

*AYE!* ALL MUST *DIE* WHO OPPOSE MY WILL! *ALL!*

THEN, CONAN'S FURY IS HORRIBLE TO *BEHOLD*-- AS HE LIFTS THE AGE-OLD SORCERER, LIKE SOME SMALL, WHIMPERING *RODENT*--

CALL OFF YOUR DEMON, WIZARD--OR I'LL---

*NEVER! NEVER!*

*BAH!* YOU'RE HARDLY *WORTH* THE KILLING.

STILL, I'D TEND TO YOU-- IF I HAD THE *TIME.*

BUT NOW, *I* MUST DO WHAT YOU WILL *NOT*--

I MUST SAVE THE *GIRL!*

DO YOU HEAR, BARBARIAN? DO YOU *HEAR?*

SHE *LIVES*-- BUT YOU HAVE TAKEN MY DAUGHTER'S *HEART* FROM ME---

AND IT CAN NEVER BE WHOLLY *MINE* AGAIN.

IT IS A *LONELY* THING--AND *MADDENING*--

--TO BE THE *LAST* OF A ONCE-PROUD RACE, AND TO BE *FOR-SAKEN* BY THE ONLY ONE YOU HOLD DEAR.

AND *SO*--

"*BEWARRRE*"

GONE-- BOTH OF THEM.

IF THEY WERE EVER TRULY *HERE*.

BUT THEY WERE *REAL* ENOUGH, IT SEEMS--FOR THE CASTLE STILL STANDS, AND *GOLDEN COINS* YET STUD THE FLOOR WHERE THEY HAVE FALLEN---

...*FIFTY* GOLD PIECES, THEIR GLITTER BLINDING THE CIMMERIAN TO THOUGHTS OF A DEMON--A WIZARD--- AND A GIRL WHO OFFERED HIM--*IMMORTALITY.* A GIRL WHO---

BUT *NO*-- IT IS BETTER TO COUNT THE *GOLD*--TO RECALL THAT MORE OR LESS THIS SUM WAS OFFERED HIM TO *SLAY* ZUKALA.

YET, ISN'T THE MAN-WIZARD *VANISHED*--AND ISN'T THAT THE SAME THING?

*NO* NEED TO BOTHER GOING BACK TO THE *VILLAGE*--NO NEED AT *ALL*---

--NOT WHEN THE ROAD TO SIN-DRENCHED *SHADIZAR* WINDS BY THE THE FOOT OF THE HILL--!

FINIS

# CONAN THE BARBARIAN! ™

STAN LEE EDITOR • ROY THOMAS WRITER • BARRY SMITH ARTIST • SAL BUSCEMA INKER • MIKE STEVENS LETTERER •

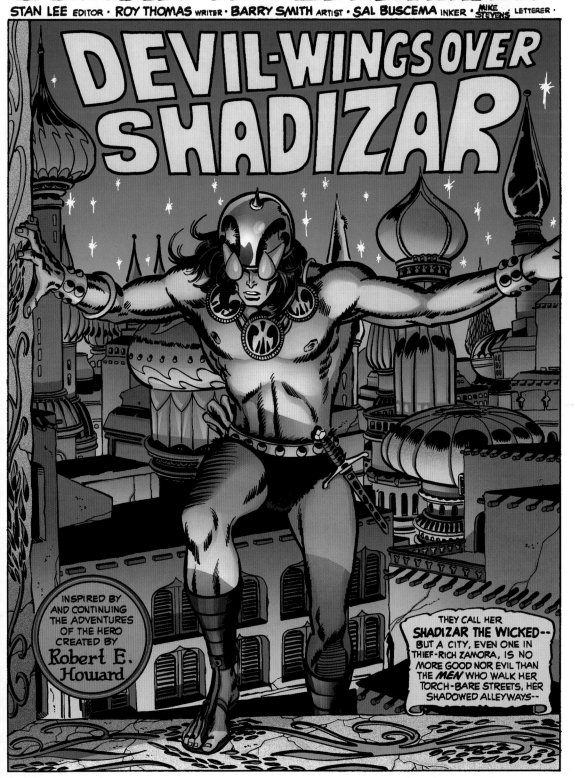

## DEVIL-WINGS OVER SHADIZAR

INSPIRED BY AND CONTINUING THE ADVENTURES OF THE HERO CREATED BY Robert E. Howard

THEY CALL HER **SHADIZAR THE WICKED**-- BUT A CITY, EVEN ONE IN THIEF-RICH ZAMORA, IS NO MORE GOOD NOR EVIL THAN THE *MEN* WHO WALK HER TORCH-BARE STREETS, HER SHADOWED ALLEYWAYS--

--OR WHO CLAMBERS SILENTLY OVER WALLS THAT HAVE WITNESSED A THOUSAND GRISLY ACTS...

NO WONDER THEY CALL YOU *BLACKRAT.* YOU'RE ALWAYS NOSING ABOUT WHERE YOU DON'T BELONG.

MAYBE SO-- BUT *I'M* THE ONE WHO *STABBED* HIM.

AFTER ALL, WASN'T *I* THE ONE WHO *SUBDUED* THE OLD GOLDSMITH *?*

BESIDES, HOW CAN *TWO* MEN DIVIDE *THREE* GOLD OBJECTS?

THE SAME WAY *ONE* MAN CAN DIVIDE *ANOTHER* MAN *!*

NO NEED FOR TWO FRIENDS TO *QUARREL.*

LET *ME* SETTLE IT-- BY *TAKING* THAT THIRD PIECE!

MITRA!

I'M *WARNING* YOU, FAFNIR --I WANT MY PROPER *SHARE* OF THE BOOTY.

YOU *WRONG* ME, LITTLE ONE, AS ALWAYS.

HAVEN'T I OFFERED YOU THE GOLDEN *GOBLET* WE STOLE *?*

WHILE *YOU* KEEP BOTH THE CANDLE-STICK *AND* THE DAGGER, I SUPPOSE.

I DON'T KNOW WHO YOU *ARE,* BARBARIAN --

BUT MY *BLADE* WILL TEACH YOU THE FOLLY OF LEAPING *SWORD-LESS* INTO A DISPUTE.

HURRY UP AND *RUN HIM THRU,* RODENT-- BEFORE HE DIES OF *OLD AGE!*

ALWAYS *BOSSING* ME, AREN'T YOU, FAFNIR *?*

I'VE HALF A A MIND TO LET THE YOUNG SWINE *LIVE,* JUST FOR SPITE.

BY MITRA, DO I HAVE TO *SHOVE* HIM ONTO YOUR--

AARRRAMH!

FAFNIR! HE--HE *DUCKED.!!*

JUST AS *YOU* SHOULD HAVE DONE, DOG!

GOBLET, CANDLE-STICK, AND DAGGER, ALL OF *GOLD*--- JUST AS THEY SAID.

I SHOULD TAKE THEM *BACK* TO THAT GOLD-SMITH---

NO--HE'S DOUBTLESS *DEAD*.

WELL, TO HIS *HEIRS*, THEN.

BUT I DON'T KNOW WHO THEY *ARE*.

BESIDES, THEY'D PROBABLY JUST *SQUANDER* THE GOLD.

*HUHNN!* ALL THIS PONDERING MAKES MY *HEAD* SPIN.

MAYBE A FLAGON OF *WINE* WILL HELP ME SORT THINGS OUT.

*WELCOME*, OUT-LANDER, TO THE HOUSE OF *SUWONG*. YOU ARE WISE NOT TO WANDER THE CITY AT NIGHT.

THE STREETS ARE NOT *SAFE* FOR A LONE MAN--- WITH A *MONEY-SACK* IN HIS BELT.

SO I'VE *HEARD*.

*TAKING A DEEP BREATH, THE YOUNG BARBARIAN FROM THE NORTH ENTERS THE SINGLE FUME-CHOKED ROOM WHICH MAKES UP THE TAVERN -- A SLEEK HILL-PANTHER STRIDING CONFIDENTLY INTO A KENNEL WHERE JACKALS ARE BRED---*

SO YOU'D *LIKE* A DROP, EH, LAD?

WELL, WE TAKE ONLY *GOLD COINS* HERE.

NONE OF YOUR WEASEL-PELTS OR *MUSK-OX HORNS*...

I *HAVE* GOLD-- CANNOT YOU *SEE*?

NOW, WILL YOU *SERVE* ME AT ONCE, OR---

*A VEILED THREAT*---AND THE LUSTRE OF FRESH-MINTED *COINS*. WHAT ZAMORIAN BARTENDER COULD RESIST SUCH A BLEND? THUS, ERE LONG---

A THOUSAND PARDONS, SIR---BUT MAY I *SPEAK* WITH YOU FOR A MOMENT?

YOU'VE SPIED ON ME LIKE A *HAWK* SINCE I CAME IN.

*SIT* WITH ME--- AND SAVE YOUR *EYES*.

MY *THANKS*, WAYFARER. I *WORK* HERE--- AND I GET TIRED OF STANDING.

*JENNA* IS MY NAME. HAVE *YOU* ONE?

I AM *CONAN*--- A CIMMERIAN.

*CIMMERIA*? I THOUGHT THAT LAND WAS ONLY A *LEGEND*---

---LIKE *AESGAARD*, AND *VANAHEIM*--- AND *ATLANTIS*, WHICH MEN SAY SANK BENEATH THE SEA.

I WAS IN *AQUILONIA* ONCE, THOUGH. I EVEN SAW *KING NUMEDIDES* HIMSELF, IN HIS ROYAL CHARIOT.

I'VE *HEARD* OF AQUILONIA-- BUT NOT OF ITS *KING*.

DO YOU *LIKE* TO MAKE JOURNEYS?

OH YES--- WHEN I GET THE *CHANCE*.

BUT THAT TAKES *MONEY* --SO MOSTLY I STAY IN *SHADIZAR*.

MONEY'S NOT SO HARD TO COME BY. MONTHS AGO, I LEFT MY HOMELAND *PENNILESS*---

--- BUT I HAD A BIT OF LUCK WITH A *WIZARD* RECENTLY---AND EARLIER TONIGHT, I ---

TELL ME, IS SHADIZAR ALWAYS SO *NOISY?*

*THIS?* TONIGHT, OUR CITY IS LIKE ONE *DEAD.*

WHAT HAVE YOU IN THE POUCH?

OH, *THAT!* JUST A FEW *SWEET-MEATS,* AND--

*LOOK OUT!*

I'LL PUT UP WITH THIS *NO* LONGER, KUSHITE. IF YOU AND YOUR FRIEND *MUST* HAVE YOUR WRESTLING MATCH-- TAKE IT *OUTSIDE!*

DON'T CALL ME A *KUSHITE!*

I'M NO *KUSHITE* DOG-- NO SAVAGE EATER OF *CARRION*-- -- BUT A FULL-BLOODED PRINCE OF *ZEMBABWEI.*

*AYE?* WELL, COME ONE STEP *CLOSER*--

-- AND I'LL CROWN YOU PRINCE OF *HELL!*

EASY, MY FRIEND. WHY DO YOU NOT *SHEATHE* YOUR WEAPON?

MY *TEMPER* FLARES LIKE THE MANE OF A LION.

WE WANT NO *TROUBLE*, DO WE, NUBION?

PERHAPS WE *SHOULD* TAKE OUR SPORTING ELSEWHERE.

I --- HAVE ALL YOUR *SWEET-MEATS*, CONAN.

THEN *LET* THESE TWO STAY HERE AND FINISH CRACKING EACH OTHER'S BONES.

WE'LL GO WHERE A MAN AND A MAID MAY TALK IN *PEACE*.

CROM'S DEVILS! I'LL NEVER UNDER-STAND THIS THING CALLED *CIVILIZATION*.

SMALL WONDER, THEN, THAT YOU *LEFT*.

WHY DID YOU *LIE* TO ME ABOUT WHAT WAS IN THAT POUCH?

IN MY HOMELAND, EACH WARRIOR SITS IN *SILENCE*... AND SIPS HIS BREW *ALONE*.

THERE WERE *SOLDIERS* ABOUT---PERHAPS EVEN MEMBERS OF THE *PALACE GUARD*.

THEY MADE ME *NERVOUS*.

I SEE. THEY MIGHT ASK HOW A *BARBARIAN* CAME BY SO MUCH GOLD--

-- ESPECIALLY WHEN AN OLD GOLDSMITH WAS *ROBBED* AND *MURDERED* EARLIER TONIGHT.

OH-- COULD WE GO IN *HERE* FOR A MOMENT, CONAN?

*JENNA*, MY SYLPH-LIKE STAR-- YOU BRIGHTEN AN OLD MAN'S *SKY*.

AND *YOU* ARE A SHAMELESS *FLATTERER*.

COME, CONAN-- I WANT YOU TO MEET *MALDIZ*--

--THE FINEST *BLACKSMITH* IN SHADIZAR, EVEN IF HE *IS* MY UNCLE.

YOU, UH, MAKE ME *BLUSH*, MY DEAREST NIECE.

BUT, WHO'S THIS YOUNG *BLADE* WITH YOU?

HIS NAME IS *CONAN*, UNCLE.

HE HAS *GOLD* YOU MUST *MELT DOWN*--AND RECAST IN THE SHAPE OF A *HEART*.

*WHAT?*

HMMM--- SHE'S CAUGHT *YOU* AS OFF-GUARD AS *ME*, EH, LAD?

BUT SHE'S *RIGHT*, YOU KNOW--AT LEAST IF THE GOLD CAME FROM WHERE I *SUSPECT*.

YES... ALL RIGHT, JENNA...

*PLEASE*, CONAN---?

THEN JUST SET ASIDE FIVE GOLD COINS FOR OLD *MALDIZ*, YOUTH.

*THIS* WON'T TAKE LONG.

*TOO* LONG, FOR YOUNG EYES WHICH *BURN* INTO EACH OTHER--BUT FINALLY--

*HERE* YOU GO, MY FRIEND.

NOT QUITE UP TO A *FALCON* I ONCE FORGED! STILL--

*WAIT.* LET ME *COOL IT* OFF FOR YOU.

I SUPPOSE-- IT'S *BEAUTIFUL*, BUT--

YES-- *BEAUTIFUL*--!

THEN GO IN *PEACE*, CHILDREN.

JENNA, YOU COME SEE ME *AGAIN* SOON, EH?

OF *COURSE*, DEAR UNCLE. FAREWELL.

*THE DARK OF THE MOON*: A TIME FOR YOUNG LOVERS, IN THE SHADOWED GROVES NEAR SHADIZAR---

WAS THERE TRULY NEED TO RECAST *ALL* MY GOLD, GIRL?

IT *DOES* MAKE IT HARDER TO *SPEND*.

BUT EASIER TO *CARRY*, DON'T YOU THINK?

TO CARRY? YES, BUT *I* HARDLY NEED--

THEN, YOU REALLY OUGHT TO *THANK* ME-- OUGHTN'T YOU---?

YES-- I GUESS I *SHOULD!*

*HUH?* WHY DID YOU PUSH ME *AWAY?* I THOUGHT--

AND *I* THOUGHT YOU KNEW HOW TO *TREAT* A WOMAN.

I AM A *GIRL*--NOT SOME *BEAR* THAT YOU ARE WRESTLING.

BESIDES, THOSE *HORNS* ON YOUR *HELMET* BRUISED MY FOREHEAD.

THERE, *THAT'S* BETTER.

IT MAKES YOU LOOK LIKE A *YAK*, ANYWAY.

NOW *GENTLY...* GENTLY...

AS GENTLY, PERHAPS, AS THE TREAD OF MUFFLED *SOLES* ON NIGHT-COOL *SANDS*---?

THAT'S NOT *TOO* BAD. NOW, IF ONLY--

OHHH--!

WHAT'S *WRONG*, GIRL? WHAT ARE YOU *LOOKING*--

*HAH!* THIS ONE IS A *HELLCAT*-- BUT WE CAN TAME HER.

STRIKE THE BARBARIAN *AGAIN*. HE KNOWS NOT HOW TO *FALL*.

*NO?* THEN, BY THE *NIGHT-GOD* WE ALL DO SERVE--

--WE'LL *TEACH* HIM SOON ENOUGH!

DARKNESS SWALLOWS DARKNESS-- BLACK ENGULFS BLACK-- THE NIGHT BECOMES A SEA TO *DROWN* IN--

BUT A CIMMERIAN'S HARD-BONED *SKULL* IS A WONDER UNTO ITSELF-- AND THUS, ERE LONG--

THE RED-ROBED ONES LEFT THE *GOLDEN HEART* IN ITS POUCH--

--AND TOOK, INSTEAD, THE *GIRL*.

I SWEAR BY *CROM*--

--STRANGE ARE THE WAYS OF *SHADIZAR!*

EH? WHO IS IT THIS T--

OH, IT'S YOU, BARBARIAN. WHERE IS--

YOUR NIECE HAS BEEN TAKEN, MALDIZ.

UNKNOWN MEN STRUCK ME FROM BEHIND-- AND I AWOKE TO FIND HER GONE!

THEN WE TWO SHALL FIND HER, CONAN-- OR MITRA IS NOT IN HIS HEAVEN!

QUICKLY--- DID YOU SEE YOUR ATTACKERS?

THEY WILL BE EASY TO FIND-- IF THEY STILL WEAR THE RED ROBES THIS CAME FROM.

THEY SERVE SOMETHING CALLED-- THE NIGHT-GOD.

RED ROBES? NIGHT-GOD?

FORGET HER, LAD.

SHE IS-- AS GOOD AS DEAD.

I DON'T KNOW WHAT YOU MEAN-- BUT HOW CAN YOU SAY TO FORGET HER, MAN?

YOUR OWN NIECE--

I HAVE NO NIECE, STRIPLING!

THAT IS BUT A GAME SHE PLAYS-- JENNA LIES MUCH, YOU KNOW.

AND I LET HER LIE, BECAUSE I AM FOND OF HER.

BUT I'D HELP YOU SAVE HER-- IF ANY MAN COULD.

COME-- FOLLOW ME--

AND I'LL SHOW YOU WHY NO ONE CAN.

ONCE EACH MONTH, IN THE DARK OF THE MOON, A YOUNG GIRL VANISHES FROM OUR STREETS.

WE KNOW THAT THE DEVOTEES OF THE NAMELESS NIGHT-GOD TAKE HER THERE-- TO THAT MINARET.

A SMALL PRICE TO PAY-- FOR PEACE WITH A DARK AND SINISTER GOD!

BUT-- WHY IS THE DOME OPEN?

ONLY THE WORSHIPPERS OF THE *NIGHT-GOD* KNOW THAT, LAD.

AND THEY'RE NOT LIKELY TO *SAY,* ARE THEY?

SO NOW YOU SEE *WHY* YOU MUST FORGET POOR JENNA, DON'T YOU, CONAN?

CONAN??

OPEN TO THE PIT-BLACK *SKY* IT YAWNS, LIKE THE GAPING MAW OF SOME GREAT *CARNIVORE--ITS* CRIMSON-COWLED PUPS ALL SAFE WITHIN...

--BUT FOR *ONE* GRIM VOTARY, WHO HAS LINGERED *O'ERLONG* AT SOME UNTOLD DEED--

--AND NOW--

--MUST PAY THE *PRICE!*

**EVEN NOW, CONAN COULD HARDLY EXPLAIN WHY HE HAS COME HERE--**

**--HERE, TO THE VERY *DEN* OF THE MOST FEARED SECT IN ALL OF SIN-WRACKED *SHADIZAR* --**

**--TO TRY TO SAVE THE LIFE OF A WENCH HE HARDLY *KNOWS* -- OR *PERISH* IN THE TRYING.**

**BUT HER YOUNG LIPS WERE *WARM* -- HER LAUGHTER LIKE SMALL SILVER *BELLS* -- AND--**

**BELLS! THE CIMMERIAN HEARS THEIR MOMENTARY ECHO, FROM SOMEWHERE IN THE SPRAWLING TEMPLE--**

**BUT WHERE? WHERE ??**

YOU ARE *LATE*, FELLOW.

HAVE YOU NO *EARS*? THE CEREMONY IS ABOUT TO--

HOLD!

*YOU* ARE NO *TRUE* ACOLYTE OF THE NIGHT-GOD.

ONLY THOSE WITH EYES WHERE *MID-NIGHT* DWELLS MAY SERVE HIM.

YET-- TOUCH *NOT* YOUR SWORD-HILT.

I'LL TELL NO ONE.

NO, NOR SHALL *YOU* TELL ANY *TAVERN ROGUES* WHAT YOUR CURIOUS EYES MAY BEHOLD THIS NIGHT.

FOR, WHO LISTENS TO THE RAVINGS OF A *MAN MADE MAD?*

HURRY, FOOL.

THE CEREMONY *BEGINS.*

THE PRIESTESS *HAJII* RECITES THE INCANTATION.

*GATHER, ROBED ONES* -- YE KEEPERS OF FLAME AND FAITH --

THE HOUR IS COME 'ROUND ONCE MORE WHEREIN WE MAKE *SACRIFICE* TO THE DARK ONE WHOM WE WORSHIP.

AND CONAN SEES THAT THE SACRIFICE IS -- *JENNA!*

BUT HIS LIPS MUST KEEP BENUMBED *SILENCE.*

O *NIGHT-GOD* -- THOU WHOM WE DO *SERVE,* YET NE'ER HAVE *SEEN* --

*ACCEPT* THEE NOW THIS *UNWORTHY GIFT* -- THIS SOILED AND SINFUL *OFFERING* -- THIS HUMAN *HECATOMB* --

TAKE HER *HENCE* -- FROM THIS VALE OF SORROW -- TO THE UNENDING *BLISS* OF THINE ETERNAL SHADOW, THY HEAVENLY ABODE.

COME! *COME NOW!*

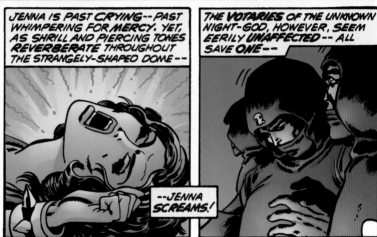

JENNA IS PAST *CRYING* -- PAST WHIMPERING FOR *MERCY.* YET, AS SHRILL AND PIERCING TONES *REVERBERATE* THROUGHOUT THE STRANGELY-SHAPED DOME --

--JENNA *SCREAMS!*

THE *VOTARIES* OF THE UNKNOWN NIGHT-GOD, HOWEVER, SEEM EERILY *UNAFFECTED* -- ALL SAVE *ONE* --

THEN, ABOVE THE DIN, THE VOICE OF *HAJI* IS HEARD: *"THE NIGHT-GOD COMETH.!"*

A *SLENDER HAND* CAPS THE SOLE LIGHTED BRAZIER -- AND THE CHAMBER IS PLUNGED INTO ABYSMAL *BLACKNESS.*

BUT STILL THE STRIDENT ECHOES OF THE BELL SEEM TO GROW LOUDER, EVER *LOUDER* -- TILL CONAN CAN STAND IT *NO LONGER.*

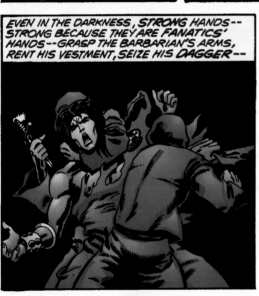

EVEN IN THE DARKNESS, *STRONG HANDS* -- STRONG BECAUSE THEY ARE *FANATICS'* HANDS -- GRASP THE BARBARIAN'S ARMS, RENT HIS VESTMENT, SEIZE HIS *DAGGER* --

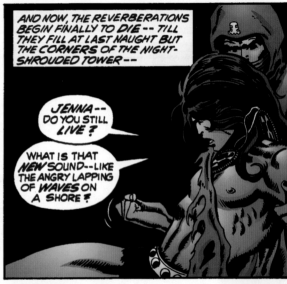

AND NOW, THE REVERBERATIONS BEGIN FINALLY TO *DIE* -- TILL THEY FILL AT LAST NAUGHT BUT THE CORNERS OF THE NIGHT-SHROUDED TOWER --

*JENNA* -- DO YOU STILL *LIVE?*

WHAT IS THAT *NEW* SOUND -- LIKE THE ANGRY LAPPING OF *WAVES* ON A SHORE?

*WINGS*, CONAN! SOMETHING HOVERS *ABOVE* ME -- FLAPPING ITS HELLISH *WINGS.*

NOW -- IT *DESCENDS* -- ITS CLAMMY FLESH TOUCHES *MINE* -- IT --

*CONAN!*

PERHAPS THE HANDS OF WILD-EYED ZEALOTS CAN HOLD HELPLESS A BEWILDERED CIMMERIAN--

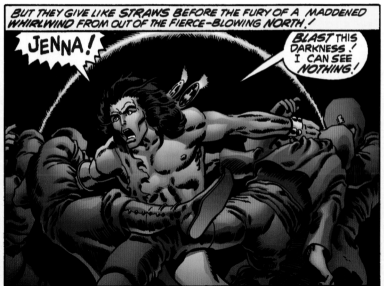

BUT THEY GIVE LIKE STRAWS BEFORE THE FURY OF A MADDENED WHIRLWIND FROM OUT OF THE FIERCE-BLOWING *NORTH* !

*JENNA!*

*BLAST* THIS *DARKNESS* ! I CAN SEE *NOTHING* !

SUDDENLY, A HIGH-PITCHED SCREECH SPLITS THE NIGHT--SOMETHING HUGE FANS THE STILL AIR--

NOW A MIGHTY BARBARIAN FIST LASHES OUT--

--SMASHING THE LOOSE-CAPPED BRAZIER--SPILLING OUT FIRE AND OIL--

--AND LIGHT--LIGHT THAT REVEALS A SCENE TO BLAST A MAN'S ETERNAL *SOUL* !

*CROM!*

OUT FROM SUNLESS CAVERNS HAS IT FLOWN, THIS TIME-FORGOTTEN NIGHT-GOD --TO PARTAKE OF A MONTHLY FOOD-OFFERING MADE IT BY PUNY CREATURES WHO NE'ER BEFORE HAVE SEEN IT--

--AND WHO, HAVING SEEN IT, WILL SCARCELY GIVE IT REASON TO COME E'ER AGAIN!

CONFUSED--BLINDED BY A FEARFULLY-WAVED BRAZIER-- THE CYCLOPEAN BEAST TURNS TOWARD THE OPEN PORTAL--

--BUT LEAVES WITH TWO WHOM IT DID NOT DESIRE!

A BABEL OF SOUNDS MINGLE IN THE EERIE DARK--

--THE SQUEAL OF THE FIRE-BLINDED NIGHT-GOD--

--THE CRIES OF RED-ROBED FIGURES, FAR BELOW--

--AND THE LONG SHRILL SHRIEK OF ONE WHO HOVERS AT THE BRINK OF MADNESS--!

HURRY, WOMAN-- BEFORE I KILL YOU--

COMMAND THIS MONSTER-THING OF YOURS TO GLIDE TO EARTH!

I-- I CANNOT! THE NIGHT-GOD KNOWS ME NOT!

I DO NAUGHT BUT SERVE IT-- I--

AIEEEE--!

FOR ONE FLEETING MOMENT, A GLEAMING TOWER LOOMS IN THE BEAST'S SKYWARD PATH--THEN--

THE BRUTE IS STILL HALF-BLINDED BY THE FLAMES I THRUST BEFORE ITS FEEBLE EYES!

THUS, PERHAPS I CAN USE THIS FIERY BRAZIER--TO GUIDE IT BEYOND THE CITY.

ALREADY IT DROPS LOWER-- LOWER-- BURDENED BY OUR TRIPLE WEIGHT.

BLASPHEMER! YOU WOULD HARM THE DARK ONE--TO SAVE A MORTAL!

IF YOU SO ENVY THE GIRL HER PLACE BENEATH THE GOD'S TALONS--

--THEN GO AND JOIN HER--!!

MAD- WOMAN!

IF I PERISH--HOW LONG DO YOU THINK YOU WILL SURVIVE!

119

CONAN-- THE GROUND COMES CLOSER-- EVER *CLOSER*--

*GOOD!* THEN PERHAPS THE GOD-BRUTE WILL *DROP* YOU--

-- WHILE IT WIPES THE TASTE OF *FIRE* FROM OUT ITS MOUTH!

SKREEEAA

LIKE A THING *CRAZED,* THE GREAT BEAST *CAROMS, COILS, CAREENS* TOWARD DESERT SOIL BELOW--

--AND TOWARD A *GROVE* OF *TREES* WHICH NEITHER IT NOR ITS HATED MAN-BURDEN *SEES*--!

ONE *LAST* BLOW, DARKLING -- AS THE *SANDS* RUSH UP TO MEET US BOTH--

NOW I *TOO* SHALL TAKE MY--

THE WORDS ARE NEVER *FINISHED* --AS SHOCK OF MASSIVE *BONE* SPLINTERS TREE AND BONE ALIKE.

A SICKENING *CRUNCH* --THE THUNDER-ING OF A MAMMOTH *FORM* PLUNGING TO EARTH -- ONE LAST, CONVULSIVE FLAPPING OF MISBEGOTTEN *WINGS* --

--THEN BOTH *MAN* AND *MONSTER* ARE STILL.

THE *NIGHT-GOD* -- IS *DEAD!*

A DEITY WORSHIPPED BY MY PEOPLE SINCE *TIME UNTOLD* --

SLAIN BY THE HAND OF SOME IGNORANT *SAVAGE!*

THE SUN AWAKENS HOT AND *SULLEN* ON THE DESERT PLAIN THAT GIRDLES THE CITY CALLED SHADIZAR...

JENNA -- ?

GONE -- WHILE I *SLEPT!*

SHE SAVED MY *LIFE* -- THEN *LEFT* ME THUS.

BUT -- SHE DID NOT GO *EMPTY-HANDED.*

A *HEART OF GOLD* -- EASIER TO *CARRY,* SHE SAID.

"*DREAM GOLDEN DREAMS,*" SHE WHISPERED.

BUT I GOT THE *DREAMS*...

...AND SHE, THE *GOLD.*

SO FARE THEE *WELL,* ANCIENT CITY.

AT LAST I KNOW WHY THEY NAMED THEE *SHADIZAR THE WICKED.*

I SHALL PASS *AGAIN* THRU YOUR GREAT BEJEWELED GATES...

...WHEN NEXT I HAVE *GOLD* THAT CAN SPARE THE LOSING.

THE DESERT SUN BURNS AWAY MEMORIES, SO THEY SAY. AYE, BARBARIAN FAR FROM HOME ...SO THEY SAY! FINIS

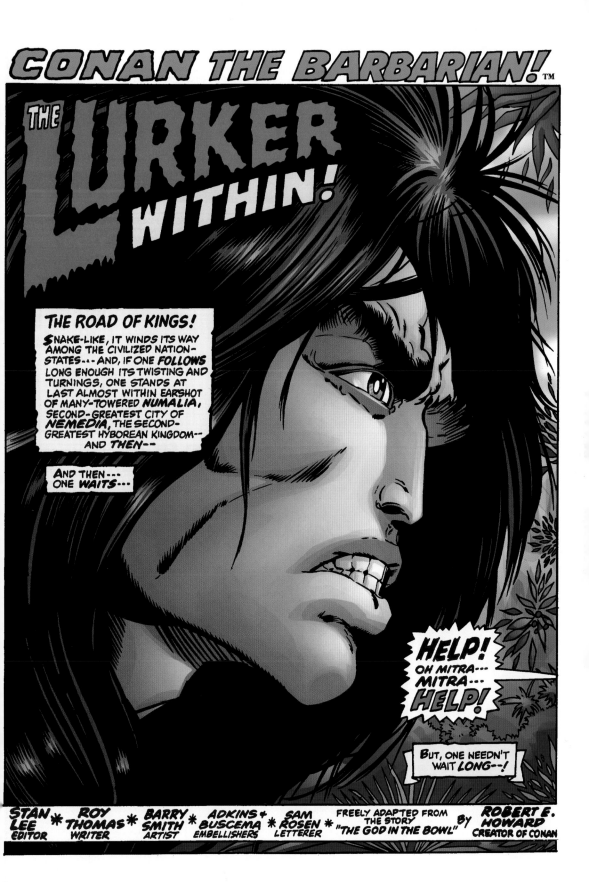

# CONAN THE BARBARIAN! ™

## THE LURKER WITHIN!

**THE ROAD OF KINGS!** SNAKE-LIKE, IT WINDS ITS WAY AMONG THE CIVILIZED NATION-STATES--- AND, IF ONE *FOLLOWS* LONG ENOUGH ITS TWISTING AND TURNINGS, ONE STANDS AT LAST ALMOST WITHIN EARSHOT OF MANY-TOWERED *NUMALIA*, SECOND-GREATEST CITY OF *NEMEDIA*, THE SECOND-GREATEST HYBOREAN KINGDOM-- AND *THEN*--

AND THEN--- ONE *WAITS*---

**HELP!** OH MITRA--- *MITRA*--- **HELP!**

BUT, ONE NEEDN'T WAIT *LONG*--!

STAN LEE EDITOR ✱ ROY THOMAS WRITER ✱ BARRY SMITH ARTIST ✱ ADKINS & BUSCEMA EMBELLISHERS ✱ SAM ROSEN LETTERER ✱ FREELY ADAPTED FROM THE STORY "THE GOD IN THE BOWL" BY ROBERT E. HOWARD CREATOR OF CONAN

ONE SWIFT *GLANCE* TELLS THE FULL STORY---

FRIGHTENED, REARING *STALLIONS*-- AN OVERTURNED *CHARIOT*, RICHLY FURNISHED--- AND A SINGLE LITHE *FIGURE*, RINGED ABOUT BY---

WOLVES!

ANOTHER MAN MIGHT *WASTE* PRECIOUS MOMENTS, DEBATING WHETHER OR NOT TO RISK HIS *LIFE* FOR SOMEONE HE HAS NEVER BEFORE SEEN ---

BUT FOR *THIS* MAN, TO *THINK* IS TO *ACT*---

TO ACT IS TO *STRIKE*---

AND TO *STRIKE*--- IS TO *KILL!*

HAH! DO THEY BREED SHARP-FANGED *JACKALS* HERE IN NEMEDIA?

BACK HOME, THERE WOULD NOW BE THREE DEAD *WOLVES* ---OR ONE DEAD *CIMMERIAN.*

DID I --- **HEAR** YOU ARIGHT?

ARE YOU TRULY A **CIMMERIAN** -- ONE OF THOSE FIERCE-EYED **BARBARIANS** FROM OUT OF THE NORTHLAND?

IF I WERE ONE OF YOUR **CIVILIZED** PALE-BLOODS, WENCH, YOU'D NOW BE A FEAST FOR THOSE **WOLVES**.

DON'T CALL ME A **WENCH!**

JUST RIGHT MY **CHARIOT** AGAIN -- AND I'LL BE ON MY **WAY**.

YOU SCREAM FOR **HELP** ONE MINUTE-- AND GIVE **ORDERS** THE NEXT, EH?

WELL, PER-HAPS I **WILL** RIGHT IT--

-- FOR REASONS-- ⌇HUHNN⌇ -- ALL MY **OWN!**

BUT, THERE WAS--- SOMETHING **BENEATH** YOUR PRECIOUS CHARIOT.

OH-- THAT'S JUST MY **DRIVER**--!

THEN-- **YOU** WILL CONDUCT ME BACK TO THE GATES OF **NUMALIA**, BARBARIAN.

HAVE YOU EVER **HANDLED** A TEAM AND CHARIOT BEFORE?

NO---**NEVER**---

BUT MAYBE **NOW** IS THE TIME TO **LEARN**.

NOT BAD --- FOR A **NOVICE**. BUT DO NOT PUT ON **AIRS** -- FOR I KNOW **WHY** YOU SAVED MY LIFE.

OH?

OBVIOUSLY, YOU WISH TO PASS THRU THE GUARDED **GATES** OF NUMALIA.

BY **YOURSELF**, YOU MIGHT GET A SPEAR IN THE BELLY -- AT LEAST A KICK IN THE **BACKSIDE**.

AH, BUT AS MY **COMPANION** -- NAY, AS MY DOCILE **DRIVER** --

WELCOME **BACK**, LADY AZTRIAS.

-- YOU MAY ENTER THE CITY IN **FINE STYLE**.

YOU'VE KEEN EYES AND A QUICK MIND -- FOR A **WOMAN**.

WHAT **ELSE** DO YOU --- **KNOW** ABOUT ME?

I WOULD **WAGER** MUCH THAT YOU ARE, BY PROFESSION -- A **THIEF**.

AND **THAT** IS SOMETHING I MUST **DISCUSS** WITH YOU, BARBARIAN --

-- IF EVER WE ESCAPE THE **HORDES** WHICH CHOKE THE CITY'S MAIN PASSAGE.

THEN -- **ENOUGH** OF THAT AVENUE OF SNAILS!

WE'LL GO **THIS** WAY --- AND **DEVIL** TAKE ANY WHO WOULD ---

CROM!

=UNNH!= MY CHARIOT'S **WHEEL** -- ITS **BRAND-NEW**!

YOURS HAS **CRACKED** IT!

YOU'LL **PAY** FOR THIS, YOU WILD-MANED SAVAGE -- **MARK** ME!

I'LL MARK YOU WITH MY **SWORD**, PIG, IF YOU DON'T ---

**HERE** NOW! WHAT'S THIS **UPROAR**?

IT'S **DIONUS**, PREFECT OF THE CITY GUARD, WHO WANTS TO KNOW!

STAY YOUR SPEAR, MAN! THIS IS BETWEEN THE *FAT ONE* AND MYSELF.

HE-- HE'S GOING TO *KILL* ME!

RUN HIM *THRU*, YOU FOOL--- *SLAY HIM!*

YES, SIRE-- I--

IN *CIMMERIA*, WE FIGHT WITH OUR *BLADES*, PREFECT--

--NOT WITH OUR *JAWS!*

STOP--ALL OF YOU! THIS MAN IS *MY* DRIVER-- *NEW* TO THE WAYS OF THE CITY.

LADY *AZTRIAS*? I-- DID NOT *SEE* YOU.

VERY WELL-- I'LL *FORGET* THIS MATTER, MY LADY-- SINCE THE SAVAGE IS IN *YOUR* KEEPING--

--THOUGH *DEMETRIO* WOULD *SKIN* ME FOR IT, IF HE KNEW.

GO ON YOUR WAY.

WHO *WAS* THAT BAD-TEMPERED DOG, GIRL?

"THE RICH, CORPULENT ONE IS *KALLIAN*--OWNER OF NUMALIA'S *HALL OF RELICS*---

"-- AND THE *BEARDED* ONE IS *DIONUS*-- STUPID, SWINISH, CRUEL.

WHICH ONE? I SAW *THREE* SUCH.

CIVIL TO ME, OF COURSE. THERE ARE *SOME* ADVANTAGES STILL TO BEING *NIECE* TO A GOVERNOR.

YET, THERE ARE *OTHER* ILLS THAT NAUGHT BUT *MONEY* WILL CURE.

COME. I HAVE SOME-THING TO *SHOW* YOU.

*THAT?* WHAT IS IT?

KALLIAN'S FAR-FAMED *HOUSE OF RELICS*--- WHERE ANTIQUITIES OF *MANY LANDS* ARE KEPT-- TREASURES WORTH A *KING'S RANSOM*--

--OR THE *GAMBLING DEBTS* OF A GOVERNOR'S NIECE!

I SHALL TELL YOU A SHORT BUT GRIPPING *TALE*, MY BARBARIAN.

WHEN YOU SAVED ME, I HAD GONE RIDING OUTSIDE THE GATES TO *THINK* CLEARLY ABOUT SOMETHING---

"---ABOUT A CARAVAN, ARRIVED THIS MORN FROM DARK STYGIA FAR TO THE SOUTH---

YOU WISH TO LEAVE THAT ANCIENT BOWL HERE OVERNIGHT? WHY?

'TIS A GIFT FROM ONES WHO MUST BE NAME-LESS--

--TO KARANTHES OF HANUMAR, PRIEST OF THE GOD-BIRD IBIS.

AYE! OTHER HANDS WILL CARRY IT TO THAT CITY ON THE MORROW.

BUT WE HAVE BUSI-NESS ELSE-WHERE, AND MUST BE GONE AT ONCE.

"RICH AS FABLED KRASSUS IS OLD KALLIAN--BUT STILL THE THOUGHT OF WHAT MIGHT LIE WITHIN THE GREAT LOCKED BOWL PLAGUED HIM---

LADY AZTRIAS, I SORROW THAT I CAN-NOT HELP YOU--WITH THAT MONETARY MATTER.

PERHAPS IF YOU DARED SPEAK OF IT TO YOUR UNCLE, HE---

HMMM. WHAT WOULD MEN OF PAGAN STYGIA SEND TO THE PRIEST OF IBIS?

IT WAS GIVEN THE CARAVANERS, THEY SAY, BY MASKED ONES---

--WHO VOWED IT HOLDS A PRICE-LESS RELIC FOUND AMONG DEEP-SUNKEN TOMBS--

--AND WHO SAID THEY WISHED IT TO REACH WISE OLD KARANTHES--

"--BECAUSE OF THE LOVE WHICH THE SENDER BEARS THE PRIEST OF IBIS!

"KALLIAN BELIEVES THE BOWL CONTAINS AN INCOMPARABLE TREASURE-- WEALTH BEYOND HIS WILDEST DREAMS--"

--AND SO DO I! WHAT IS YOUR NAME, BARBARIAN?

I AM CONAN.

IT IS GOOD THAT I SHOULD KNOW YOUR NAME, CONAN--

--BECAUSE TONIGHT-- WHEN THE HAUNTED HUSH OF MIDNIGHT LIES HEAVY ON THE LAND---

--YOU SHALL STEAL THE CONTENTS OF THAT GREAT BOWL--FOR ME!

HUHN?

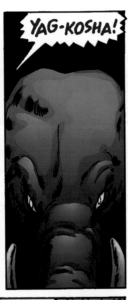

YAG-KOSHA!

BUT, 'TIS **NOT** THE ALIEN **GOD**-THING WHOM ONCE HE SLEW IN FAR-OFF **ZAMORA**---

NO, MERELY A **REAL** ELEPHANT-- AND **STUFFED,** IN THE BARGAIN!

NOW, SILENTLY, UNERRINGLY, YOUNG CONAN SEEKS OUT A DOORWAY MARKED WITH THE SIGN OF **STYGIA**---

ЅƗꝞⱶΔ

--ONLY TO FIND THERE---

KALLIAN-- **DEAD!**

--AT THE VERY FOOT OF THE **BOWL** I SOUGHT!

THE BOWL IS OPEN-- **EMPTY!**

SOME **OTHER** THIEF BEAT ME **TO** IT, NO DOUBT.

NOTHING TO DO THEN, BUT--

**WHAT?** WHO THE **DEVIL**--?

STAND WHERE YOU **ARE**--OR MY NEXT ARROW PIERCES YOUR **HEART!**

THEN--- **YOU'RE** THE ONE KILLED **KALLIAN!**

EH?

DON'T TRY TO **CONFUSE** ME, FOOL.

I AM **ARUS**-- KALLIAN'S **NIGHTWATCH!**

IT IS **YOU** WHO ARE THE **MURDERER** HERE---

--- AND **GLAD** WILL BE THE **CITY GUARD** THAT I HAVE **CAPTURED** YOU!

SOUNDS: FIRST THE STRIDENT CLANG OF *BELL* -- THEN THE ROLLING THUNDER OF *HOOF* AND *WHEEL*...

WHAT *DEVIL'S WORK* IS AFOOT, WATCHMAN?

*DEMETRIO!* FORTUNE IS TRULY *WITH* ME.

THE CITY GUARD COME SWIFTLY -- AND THE *CHIEF INQUISITOR* AMONG THEM!

I WAS MAKING THE ROUNDS WITH *DIONUS* HERE, WHEN... *ISHTAR!*

THE *MASTER* OF THE HOUSE HIMSELF -- *DEAD!*

AYE -- AND MOST FOULLY *MURDERED* -- STRANGLED, I'D SAY.

*WHAT?* THEN *SEIZE THAT BARBARIAN,* GUARDSMEN.

*MOVE,* YOU LAGGARDS!

*THERE'S YOUR KILLER,* DEMETRIO.

ONLY TODAY, I HEARD HIM *THREATEN KALLIAN* -- HE INSULTED *ME* AS WELL.

*SPEAK UP,* HEATHEN! WHY DID YOU...

LET GO OF ME.

I SAID -- *LET GO!*

BY CROM, ANY MAN WHO *TOUCHES* ME AGAIN WILL QUICKLY GREET HIS ANCESTORS IN *HELL.*

*EASY,* FELLOW. YOU ARE NOT YET *ACCUSED* OF THIS CRIME.

STILL, THERE ARE *QUESTIONS* I MUST PUT YOU.

SUCH AS -- *WHY* CAME YOU HERE, IF *NOT* TO KILL THAT MAN?

I CAME -- TO *STEAL.*

TO STEAL *WHAT?*

FOOD.

YOU *LIE!* YOU KNEW THERE'D BE NO FOOD *HERE.*

*ARUS*--- COULD ANY *OTHER* MAN HAVE DONE THE DEED-- AND SNEAKED *PAST* YOU?

NOT A *CHANCE*, MY *LORD*--

STILL, I'LL GO SEARCH THIS *NEXT* CHAMBER -- AND THE ONES *ABOVE*---

--TO BE *SURE* THERE'S NO *ACCOMPLICE* LURKING ABOUT.

WE MUST ASSUME YOUR *GUILT*, BARBARIAN --- UNLESS YOU PROVE YOUR *INNOCENCE.*

BEST TELL THE *TRUTH* OF WHY YOU CAME HERE, OR---

ALL RIGHT-- WHY *NOT?* I CAME TO *STEAL* THE CONTENTS OF THAT GREAT *BOWL*--

--A GIFT FROM AN UN-KNOWN *STYGIAN* TO SOMEONE CALLED *KARANTHES*--

--PRIEST OF A GOD CALLED *IBIS.*

BUT I FOUND THE BOWL *OPEN* THUS -- AND KALLIAN *STRANGLED.*

WHY WOULD A *STYGIAN* SEND A GIFT TO A PRIEST OF *IBIS?*

THEY WORSHIP THE SERPENT-GOD *SET* IN STYGIA-- HE WHO COILS AMONGST THE OLD *TOMBS*--

--AND *SET* AND *IBIS* HAVE BEEN *FOES* SINCE THE EARTH'S FIRST DAWN--!

LET ME *PASS.* I AM *AZTRIAS* -- NIECE TO THE GOVERNOR.

OHH! MY GOOD FRIEND KALLIAN--- *DEAD!*

CONAN, CONAN-- HOW *COULD* YOU--?

YOU *KNOW* THIS MAN?

HE IS MY NEW *DRIVER*-- BUT HE AND KALLIAN *QUARRELED* ON THE STREET THIS DAY.

WHEN CONAN VANISHED, I RUSHED STRAIGHT *HERE*-- BUT *TOO LATE*, IT SEEMS!

WHILE, IN A NIGHTED CHAMBER NOT FAR DISTANT---

!

YOU LYING *WITCH!* YOU KNOW *FULL WELL* WHY I AM HERE--!

WE'VE ALL THE *PROOF* WE *NEED.* COME *ALONG*, YOU!

*DIONUS*--!

LAY ANOTHER *HAND* ON ME, DOG-- AND I'LL SPLIT YOUR *SKULL* LIKE AN OVERRIPE *PEA!*

132

WOMAN, THE *RACK* WOULD NOT HAVE TORN YOUR NAME FROM ME, IF YOU'D NOT *PANICKED*-- AND RUN HERE TO *BETRAY* ME.

BUT NOW-- *TELL* THEM HOW YOU SENT ME HERE TO STEAL-- TO PAY YOUR *GAMBLING DEBTS.*

IS THERE-- *TRUTH* TO THIS, MY LADY?

*TELL THEM!*

OH, DEMETRIO-- HOW CAN YOU EVEN *QUESTION* ME?

HE LIES. HE LIES!

IF YOU WERE A *MAN,* YOU'D NOW BE *HEADLESS,* WENCH-- OR ELSE--

AAIIEEEEEL

*ISHTAR!* THAT *SCREAM* LIKE A SOUL IN *TORMENT*--

IT CAME FROM UP *HERE*-- IN THAT *CHAMBER*-- BUT WHO-- WHAT--?

IT WAS A *MAN*--

AND YET, IT WAS LIKE -- AN *ANIMAL!*

KEEP YOUR WEAPONS TRAINED ON THE *BARBARIAN,* SWINE.

*DIONUS*-- L-LOOK!

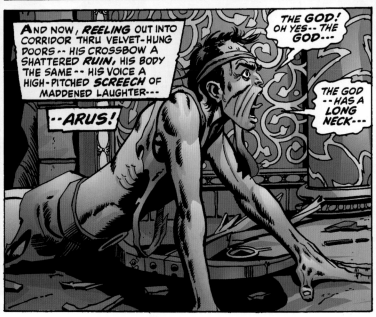

AND NOW, *REELING* OUT INTO CORRIDOR THRU VELVET-HUNG DOORS -- HIS CROSSBOW A SHATTERED *RUIN,* HIS BODY THE SAME -- HIS VOICE A HIGH-PITCHED *SCREECH* OF *MADDENED* LAUGHTER----

*--ARUS!*

THE GOD! OH YES-- THE GOD---

THE GOD --HAS A LONG NECK---

--OH, A-- CURSED-- LONG-- NECKKKK...

HE'S--*DEAD*--WITH NOT A *MARK* ON HIM!

IN MITRA'S NAME-- *WHAT IS IN THAT CHAMBER?*

*THAT,* DIONUS, IS PRECISELY WHAT I INTEND TO *FIND OUT.*

THE ROOM IS A *SHAMBLES.* ARUS FOUGHT *HARD* FOR HIS LIFE-- THOUGH NOT HARD *ENOUGH,* IT SEEMS.

AT LEAST THIS IS *ONE* MURDER WE CAN'T ACCUSE *YOU* OF COMMITTING, BARBARIAN.

MY LADY-- DO NOT LEAVE MY *SIGHT.* THERE MAY STILL BE *DANGER--*

BUT THERE IS ALSO WEALTH-- SO VERY *MUCH* WEALTH--

AYE, *WEALTH...* AND, FROM BEHIND A HEAVY GILDED SCREEN--A *FACE--*

12

--A FACE THAT WELL MIGHT BE THE MARBLED MASK OF A *GOD,* CARVED BY SOME MASTER HAND---

EXCEPT THAT---

----*THIS* MASK---

--*LIVES!*

COME.

NEITHER WEAKNESS, NOR MERCY, NOR CRUELTY, NOR KINDNESS, NOR ANY OTHER *HUMAN EMOTION* SHOWS IN THAT COLD, CLASSIC COUNTENANCE--

MY LADY...

WHAT--?

WHAT PEERLESS PERFECTION OF **BODY** THE SCREEN MUST CONCEAL -- PERFECTION TO **MATCH** THE GODLIKE FACE, THE GOLDEN VOICE---

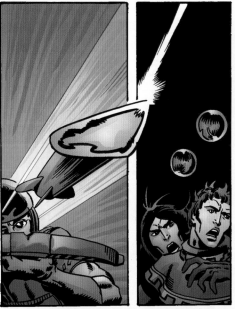

IT SPEAKS NOT **AGAIN** -- BUT WITH A THRASHING, A SHIMMERING, A SUDDEN **LUNGING OUTWARD** ---

-- IT **STRIKES!**

AND STILL, THAT **FACE** -- FULL OF LIFE, COLD AND STRANGE, BEYOND THE GRASP OF **MAN** ---

HELP ME! **HELP ME!!**

THEN -- **THIS** IS THE **MURDERER!**

A MAN-HEADED **SERPENT** -- SUCH AS MEN **WHISPER** ABOUT, IN DARK **LEGENDS!**

**RUN!!** IT IS A SON OF **SET** -- COME UP FROM **STYGIA** TO SLAY US ALL!

--- THAT FACE WHICH FILLS THE EYE WITH *BEAUTY*...

--- AND THE *SOUL* WITH NAMELESS *TERROR!*

STAND *ASIDE,* FOOL! LET ME *OUT* OF THIS PIT OF HELL!

YOU *CAN'T* FLEE, DOG-- NOT *NOW!*

*CAN'T* I? YOU JUST *WATCH* ME, BARBARIAN!

ALL RIGHT, THEN--

... I WILL WATCH YOU!

DON'T *DESPAIR,* MY LADY!

I'LL *SAVE* YOU-- FROM THIS BONE-CRUSHING *FIEND.*

COURAGE BORN OF *MADNESS!* YOU'LL BE LUCKY TO SAVE *YOUR-SELF,* MAN!

NO ANSWER--

THE THING'S CRUSHED THE *BREATH* OUT OF HIM--IF NOT *LIFE!*

136

THEN, BY CROM, I'LL DO WHAT HE COULD **NOT**--!

I'LL MAKE YOU **SCREAM!**

AND, AS INHUMAN SHRIEK IS TORN FROM GHASTLY THROAT, A STREAM OF UNEARTHLY **IMAGES** SUDDENLY FLOODS IN UPON THE EMBATTLED BARBARIAN---

--VISIONS OF A **MAN**, CLOAKED IN ROBES AND DARKNESS, TORCH CLENCHED IN BONE-WHITE FINGERS---

--SEARCHING 'MIDST GRISLY CAVERNS 'NEATH THE HAUNTED PYRAMIDS OF TIMELESS **STYGIA**--

--TILL HE FINDS--- THE **BOWL!**

FOR, THE GODS OF EONS PAST DID **NOT** DIE AS MEN DIE--- BUT FELL INTO LONG SLUMBERS, TILL WAKENED BY ONE STEEPED ENOUGH IN SORCERY TO **COMMAND** THEM--!

AND THAT ONE HAD SENT *DEATH* TO THE PRIEST OF IBIS --*COILED DEATH* THAT SPRANG FORTH AT *KALLIAN* WHEN HE LOOSED THE LID OF THE GREAT BOWL---

*DEATH* THAT CALLED ONCE TO *ARUS*, O'ER WHOSE BODY BOTH SERPENT AND CIMMERIAN NOW TUMBLE---

*DEATH* THAT, EVEN NOW, DRAWS EVER MORE *TIGHTLY* ABOUT CONAN'S STRAINING *MIDDLE*---

*DEATH* THAT, HALF-GLIMPSED, CAN MAKE A MAN *MAD!*

*DEVIL! MONSTER!* YOU TOOK MY *SWORD*-- UP TO THE *HILT*---

NOW WHY DON'T YOU *DIE*-- AS YOU HAVE *NEVER*-- DIED BEFORE!

*DIE*--- BLAST YOUR BONES--

*DIE*--!

**DIE!**

FINALLY -- TURNED ME *LOOSE* -- EH, DEVIL?

FINALLY -- TURNED ME --

-- LOOSE.

NOW, 'TIS *STILL* -- AS SILENT AS IT MUST INDEED HAVE BEEN ---

-- WITHIN THOSE DANK, DEEP *SEPULCHRES* 'NEATH STYGIAN SANDS.

BUT, AT LENGTH, SOMETHING STIRS --- *LIFE* STIRS --

AND IT IS *PAIN* THAT BIRTHS THE STIRRING--- A THROBBING IN TEMPLES THAT HAD NEARLY BURST, IN A RIGHT HAND THAT HAD BATTERED A STONE-COLD BROW---

BUT, EVEN THE PAIN IS *GOOD* TO FEEL---

FOR, THE NETHER SIDE OF PAIN--- IS *DEATH*.

AND CONAN IS ALIVE--- *ALIVE!*

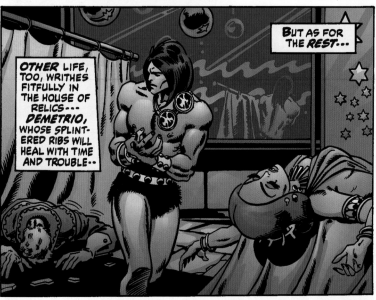

OTHER LIFE, TOO, WRITHES FITFULLY IN THE HOUSE OF RELICS--- *DEMETRIO*, WHOSE SPLINTERED RIBS WILL HEAL WITH TIME AND TROUBLE--

BUT AS FOR THE *REST*---

....DEAD.

ALL, ALL---

....DEAD!

CROM!

LIKE A MAN *POSSESSED*, YOUNG CONAN GAZES INTO THE BOWL--- AND HE KNOWS, SOMEHOW, THAT HE LOOKS UPON THE FACE AND FEATURES OF *THOTH-AMON*--

*THOTH-AMON*--- MOST FEARED OF STYGIAN WIZARDS-- HE WHO AWAKENED AND NOW COMMANDS THE SONS OF *SET*, THE SERPENT-GOD---

AND NOW, AT LAST, THE FULL *HORROR* OF IT ALL RUSHES OVER CONAN---

--AND HE *FLEES*---

THE THOUGHT OF *SET* IS LIKE A *NIGHTMARE*--- --AY, AND OF THE *CHILDREN* OF SET, WHO ONCE DID RULE THE EARTH, AND THEN DID SLEEP IN NIGHTED CAVERNS BELOW THE BLACK PYRAMIDS---

NOR DOES HE *SLACKEN* HIS HEADLONG FLIGHT---

--UNTIL THE SHIMMERING SPIRES OF THRICE-CURSED NUMALIA *FADE* INTO COMING DAWN BEHIND HIM---!

# THE KEEPERS OF THE CRYPT

THE *MOON-GOD* SQUINTS HIS ONE GOOD EYE -- AS HALF A DOZEN *TORCHES* MAKE MOTTLED ISLANDS OF LIGHT-- BUT, PROD NOT THE HIGH RICH *GRASS* FOR THE LURKING *VIPER*, SOLDIERS OF CORINTHIA--

STAN LEE
EDITOR

ROY THOMAS
WRITER

BARRY SMITH
ARTIST

SUTTON and PALMER
INKERS

SAM ROSEN
LETTERER

BASED ON AN ORIGINAL SYNOPSIS BY ROBERT E. HOWARD, CREATOR OF CONAN

FOR, 'TIS HIGH O'ERHEAD THAT DEATH DOES SMILE HIS GRIM, TIGHT SMILE --!

LESS *NOISE*, YOU *WINE-SOPS!*

DO YOU THINK WE TRAIL A *DEAF* MAN, AS WELL AS A *THIEF?*

MYSELF, CAPTAIN BURGUN -- I DON'T SEE *WHY* WE'RE TRAILING ANYBODY AT *ALL!*

BECAUSE CORINTHIA HAS A TREATY WITH *NEMEDIA*, THAT COLOSSUS TO OUR *NORTH*, FOOL.

SO WHEN OUR GOOD NEIGHBOR CRIES *FOX* -- WE LOOK TO HIS *HEN-HOUSE!*

IT SEEMS THIS *BARBARIAN* ROBBED A *HOUSE OF RELICS* ...

HAH! FOR EACH ACHING CORN, I'LL GUT THAT SAVAGE *TWICE*, WHEN WE CATCH HIM.

IF WE CATCH HIM.

HE'S DOUBTLESS *MILES* FROM THIS BORDER, BY NOW.

HO, ARI-- DID YOU *HEAR* SOMETHING?

I-I'M NOT SURE. I--

MITRA! *GREAT MITRA!*

AA!EE

NO.

**TURN AROUND, DOG-- AND MAKE READY TO DIE!**

**SURPRISED, BARBARIAN-- THAT ONE MAN ESCAPED THE FULL BRUNT OF YOUR LITTLE AVALANCHE?**

**MAYBE MY MEN WERE CUT-THROATS FROM EVERY RATHOLE IN CORINTHIA--**

**THEY STILL DE-SERVED A BET-TER MURDER THAN A--A--**

**YES, BY MITRA-- A CIMMERIAN! I KNOW YOU, DOG!**

**IT WAS AT VENARIUM I SAW YOU --JUST TWO WINTERS GONE...**

*"AYE, VENARIUM-- NORTHERNMOST OUT-POST OF MY NATIVE GUNDERLAND--- THOUGH IT'S TRUE WE HAD PUSHED OUR BORDERS NORTH A BIT---*

**LET ME HEAR THOSE CROSSBOWS SING, LADS.**

**WE'LL SHOW THOSE CIMMERIAN SCUM WHOSE LANDS THESE ARE NOW.**

*"BUT, IT WAS WE GUNDERMEN WHO LEARNED THAT DAY'S LESSON-- AND MANY LIVED TO LEARN NO OTHER..."*

"AND **YOUNG** AS YOU WERE, YOU WERE THE FIERCEST, MOST **RECKLESS** OF THAT BLOOD-CRAZED HORDE---

"IN TRUTH, I HACKED MY WAY THRU MY OWN DYING **MEN** TO GET AT YOU -- AND WE'D HAVE CROSSED SWORDS **THEN**, IF I COULD HAVE REACHED YOU THROUGH THE CARNAGE---

BUT VENARIUM **FELL**--AND I **LEFT** THE AQUILONIAN ARMY--

-- WINDING UP **HERE**, BY AND BY.

SOME JOKE ON **BOTH** OF US, EH, BARBARIAN?

NO ANSWER? THEN, STAND YOU **READY**, DOG--

--AND I'LL **SLICE** THE WORDS OUT OF YOU!

**TALK**, BLAST YOU! I'VE NO TASTE FOR DUELING WITH **SHADOWS**.

**TALK!**

TALK?

AYE, GUNDER-MAN-- I'LL EVEN PLAY A **SONG** FOR YOU---

A SHORT, **SWEET** SONG -- ON MY **BROAD-SWORD**.

AND SORRY YOUR **GHOST** SHALL BE THAT EVER YOU **HEARD** IT.

THEN, NO PAUSE -- NO BACK-CAST GLANCE -- AS THE YOUNG BARBARIAN STRIDES *EASTWARD,* TO-WARD THE COMING DAWN---

---WHICH SHEDS ITS BIRTHING GLOW UPON--*A CITY.*

HALLOOO! IS ANYONE *HOME* IN THERE?

FROM THE LOOK OF THINGS, I'D SAY *NOT*--- BUT THERE MIGHT BE A *WELL,* AND I'M THIRSTY.

SO, I'M GOING *IN*---

-- BUT *NOT*--- HUHNN-- *THIS* WAY.

AT LEAST, NOT WHILE THERE'S A *BREACH* IN THE WALL.

STRANGE I DIDN'T SEE THIS PLACE ON ANY *MAPS*---

BUT MAYBE CORINTHIA'S *MAP-MAKERS* ARE THE EQUAL OF HER *SOLDIERS.*

WORDS FULL OF *BRAVADO*--- YET EVEN SO, AN OMINOUS *TINGLING* BEGINS IN THE NAPE OF CONAN'S NECK, AS HE CLAMBERS UP AND OVER---

-- INTO A NAMELESS CITY WHERE TIME SWEEPS *SANDS* AND *MEMORIES* THRU THE ROCK-STREWN STREETS--

-- AND WHERE A STONE-GREY *GARGOYLE* SITS SILENT ATOP A SUN-CRACKED *FOUNTAIN* WAITING FOR THE WATER-BEARERS WHO SHALL NEVERMORE COME.

GUESS I'LL FIND NO WATER *HERE,* WILL I, LITTLE *DEMON?*

THE CIMMERIAN EXPECTS NO ANSWER-- YET ONE *COMES*---

A SIBILANT *WHISPER* THAT TURNS THE HEAD TOWARD RUINED COLUMNS---

-- A MIND-BLASTING *SIGHT* THAT MAKES THE BLOOD RUN COLD.

CROM!

"*DRAGON!*" OFT HAS THE YOUTHFUL WANDERER HEARD THAT WORD SINCE HE HAS TROD MAN-MADE ROADS --- YET, IT HAS EVER SEEMED A MERE *LEGEND* -- SOMETHING TO FRIGHTEN *CHILDREN* IN THE DEAD OF NIGHT ---

-- NOT A THIRTY-FOOT *MONSTER,* WITH EACH TOOTH A *SPEAR,* EACH TALON A MAN-RENDING *SCIMITAR.*

FOR TOO LONG AN INSTANT, CONAN CONSIDERS THE CHARGING BRUTE A *MIRAGE* -- A PHANTOM BORN OF SUN, AND FATIGUE, AND BONE-DRY *THIRST* ---

BUT NOW, AS AN AGE-OLD *TROUGH* IS CRUSHED BENEATH ELEPHANTINE CLAWS ---

--- THAT INSTANT *DIES!*

I'M SURE AS THE DEVIL MY *SWORD* WON'T PIERCE YOUR SCALY HIDE, DRAGON ---

BUT *SOMEWHERE* IN THIS PILE OF RACK AND RUBBLE ---

-- MAYBE I'LL FIND SOMETHING THAT *CAN.*

BUT THE **SEARCH,** SO HARRIED AND HARD---

-- SWIFTLY LEADS TO NAUGHT---

--- SAVE A **DEAD END**---

-- AND NEARLY TO---

-- **DEATH** ITSELF!

**NOW** RANT AND RAGE ALL YOU **WANT,** YOU SLIMY SON OF A SERPENT!

YOU'LL **NEVER** REACH ME UP HERE-- NOT IF I STAY---

-- UNTIL I -- STARVE---

**STARVE!** THAT GIVES ME A **THOUGHT,** MONSTER.

YOU **CHASED** ME, NO DOUBT, BECAUSE YOU'RE TIRED OF EATING **RABBITS** AND **BRUSH-RATS.**

WELL, I DON'T HAVE A **BUFFALO** TUCKED AWAY IN MY BELT---

SO HERE'S *ANOTHER* MORSEL FOR YOU TO CHEW ON!

HAH! DON'T LIKE THE *TASTE* OF IT, EH?

WELL, THEN--- MAYBE MY *BLADE*--

--WILL BE *MORE* TO YOUR LIKING!!

ITS SOFT WHITE UNDERBELLY LAID OPEN, THE GREAT REPTILE *HEAVES* ABOUT-- *CONVULSIVELY*--

---BUT SOON, AS BLOOD RUNS FREE BENEATH THE RED-EYED SUN, IT GIVES A FINAL *TWITCH*--- AND THEN IS *STILL*.

NOR DOES THE BLACK-MANED BARBARIAN *WORRY* OVER-MUCH ABOUT THE *WHY* AND THE *WHERE-FORE* OF THE DEAD DRAGON---

--SO LONG AS NO *OTHER* SERPENTINE FORM REARS ITS SNOUT AMONGST THE CRUMBLING RUINS---

BUT RATHER, HE MAKES HIS WAY TOWARD WHAT SEEMS TO BE A GREAT *TEMPLE*, HEWN OUT OF A SINGLE MONSTROUS *STONE* IN THE VERY CENTER OF THE CITY---

FOR, WHERE THERE IS A TEMPLE, EVEN A VERY *ANCIENT* ONE---

-- THERE MAY BE *PLUNDER*, AS WELL ---

NOT EVEN *LOCKED*!

WHOEVER ABANDONED THIS CITY-- LEFT IN A *HURRY.*

NOT AS HURRIEDLY AS *YOU* SHALL TAKE LEAVE OF *LIFE*, BAR-BARIAN!

*YOU!*

I GROW *TIRED* OF TRYING TO *KILL* YOU, GUNDERMAN!

THEN YOU SHOULD'VE SLICED MY *NECK*-- NOT MY ARMOR.

*WELL?* CAN YOU GIVE ME A REASON WHY I SHOULDN'T RUN YOU *THRU*--SHEATHED SWORD AND ALL?

PERHAPS.

ORNATE AS THIS PORTAL IS, THERE MAY BE *JEWELS* ENOUGH WITHIN FOR *TWO* TO CARRY.

ALL THE MORE CAUSE TO *SLAY* YOU... AND MAKE *TWO TRIPS!*

TRUE ENOUGH.

BUT, IF THERE'S A *SECOND GUARDIAN* SKULKING ABOUT THE RUINS--YOU'LL NEED A *SWORD* AT YOUR BACK.

OR DIDN'T YOU SEE THE *DRAGON* I KILLED?

I-- SAW IT. YOU'VE *MADE* YOUR POINT.

DRAW YOUR WEAPON, BUT YOU ENTER *FIRST.*

I ONLY WANT YOUR SWORD *AT* MY BACK-- NOT *IN* IT.

GUNDERMAN, I SWEAR I *WON'T* STAB YOU-- IN THE *BACK.*

NOW COME-- I HAVEN'T TALKED *OR* LISTENED SO MUCH IN A *MONTH.*

BLACK AS THE PITS OF *HELL* IN HERE--- EVEN WITH THE *DOORS* OPEN BACK THERE.

WHAT KIND OF *NETHER MAGIC*--?

BY CROM! *LIGHT!*

AND THERE'S *ANOTHER* DOOR, JUST AHEAD OF US.

AT LEAST I'VE DISCOVERED WHERE OUR *LIGHT* COMES FROM, CIMMERIAN.

I WISH WE KNEW WHAT LIES *BEYOND* IT--

THIS WHOLE CITY SENDS *SHIVERS* UP MY SPINE.

--UP *THERE!*

I'VE NEVER SEEN ANYTHING *LIKE* THIS PLACE BEFORE.

IF THERE'S NEITHER *GOLD* NOR *WATER* WITHIN-- I'M OFF FOR *ARGOS* AND THE *SEA.*

IN *THAT* EVENT, I MIGHT HAVE TO TRY *STOPPING* YOU.

BUT, TIME ENOUGH TO QUARREL *LATER.*

AYE. RIGHT NOW, THIS INNER DOOR IS--

--ROTTEN!

*ISHTAR AND MITRA!*

*GOLD-- JEWELS--* ENOUGH TO BUY EVERY THIEF IN *ZAMORA!*

151

THESE **GEMS** ALONE WILL DO WELL BY ME WHEN I REACH THE RICH **SEA-PORTS.**

WHAT OF **YOU,** GUNDER-MAN?

THERE IS-- A **GIRL...**

SHE HERSELF HAS GOLD IN **PLENTY--** BUT NOW, PERHAPS SHE'LL LOOK WITH FAVOR ON A **WANDERER--** A MERE **SOLDIER.**

--IF THE CORINTHIANS DO NOT **SLAY** ME, FOR LOSING A WHOLE TROOP OF **MEN.**

RICH **DESERTERS** LIVE LONGER THAN GOLD-POOR **CAPTAINS...**

YES. PER-HAPS THIS WEALTH WILL BUY ME **SAFETY...**

**NAY,** WRETCHED ONE! WHAT IT HAS BOUGHT YOU BOTH--- IS **AGONY** AND **DEATH!**

WHO--?

CROM!

HOLY **MITRA!**

**SO,** TRESPASSERS-- FIRST YOU WOULD DISTURB THE **SACRED SERPENT--** THEN CRY OUT FOR **SUCCOR** FROM YOUR **GODS...**

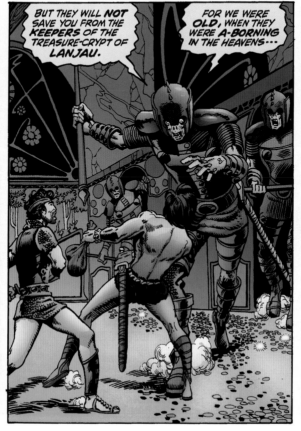

BUT THEY WILL **NOT** SAVE YOU FROM THE **KEEPERS** OF THE **TREASURE-CRYPT** OF **LANJAU.**

FOR WE WERE **OLD,** WHEN THEY WERE **A-BORNING** IN THE HEAVENS---

--AND WE SHALL SLEEP THE **DEEP SLEEP** ONCE MORE-- WHEN THEY ARE **DEAD** AND **FORGOTTEN!**

YOUNG CONAN WOULD *RUN* IF HE COULD -- OR EVEN *SCREAM*, IF IT WOULD DO ANY GOOD ---

BUT IT *WOULDN'T* --AND SO HE *LASHES OUT...*

-- WITH RESULTS *EQUALLY* FRUITLESS!

*OUT OF MY WAY*, YOU-- OR *ELSE...*

THEN, MORTALS STILL PLACE THEIR FAITH IN *MAN-FORGED BLADES?*

*FOOL!* THE VERY *GODS* DID PLACE US HERE -- TO GUARD THAT WHICH WAS *PLEASING* TO THEIR *EYE...*

--AND NO HUMAN *BLAS-PHEMER* SHALL TRANS-GRESS THESE *PORTALS* --LEST HE *DIE!*

*AIEEE!*

SO -- YOU *DO* HAVE A *SOFT SPOT*, AFTER ALL!

HO, *GUNDERMAN!* THOUGH THEIR *FLESH* BE DEAD -- THEIR *BONES* CAN BE SPLIT LIKE ANY *MAN'S!*

SEVER THE *SPINE* --AND THEY FALL LIKE *RAG DOLLS.*

DO YOU *HEAR* ME, *GUNDERMAN?*

DOES *THIS* ANSWER YOU?

*GOOD!* THEN *LET'S...*

**THEY'RE ALMOST ON *TOP* OF YOU! RUN, BARBARIAN-- IF YOU *CAN!***

**THEN *DO* IT-- IN THE NAME OF ALL THE GODS THAT *ARE!***

**AYE, BUT *FIRST*, THERE IS SOMETHING...**

**I-- CAN-- AND I *WILL*--!**

**-- THAT I MUST *DO!!***

**NOW WE GO.**

THEN, THERE IS NO MORE TIME FOR *WORDS* -- BUT ONLY FOR *FLIGHT*...

FOR, *WITHOUT* THE YAWNING PORTALS OF THE CRYPT LIES THE DAY'S BRIGHT *FREE-DOM* -- AND *LIFE* -- IF THE TWO GRIM FUGITIVES RUN *SWIFTLY* ENOUGH...

--AND IF THERE BE NO MORE *DRAGONS* IN THE OFFING...

--AND IF--

**COME, MY *BROTHERS!* THE MAN-SPAWN SHALL PAY WITH THEIR VERY *SOULS* FOR...**

HASTEN, YOUTH! THEY MUST BE HARD ON OUR---

NO! LOOK AT THEM! *LOOK!*

THEY'RE *DEAD*--- IF THEY WERE NOT DEAD *BEFORE!* NOW---

::HUHNN?::

WHAT THE *DEVIL*--?

"EARTHQUAKE!"

RUN, MAN! AND KEEP CLEAR OF ANY *WALLS.*

WISE WORDS-- BUT HOW DOES ONE AVOID WALLS IN THE MIDDLE OF A *CITY?*

FLAMES NOW-- LEAPING UP ON EVERY SIDE!

BUT-- WHAT IS THERE TO *BURN*-- IN THE CITY OF THE *DAMNED?*

MEN'S **SOULS**, PERHAPS. DON'T TALK--**FLEE!**

**AYE.** WE'LL MEET BY WHAT'S LEFT OF THE **GATE**---

--IF MEET AGAIN WE **DO!**

**DESTRUCTION:** ONE FINAL, ALL-CONSUMING ORGY OF **CHAOS**, AS STONE **BULWARKS** LEAP AND DANCE AND FALL---

THEN: THE **STILLNESS.**

AND FINALLY, **AMONGST** THE **STILLNESS**---

...**LIFE.**

BUT LIFE, IT SEEMS, ONLY FOR **ONE**--- ONLY FOR **CONAN**--- NOT FOR--- FOR---

THE **NAME** HAS FOLLOWED THE **MAN**--INTO OBLIVION.

THE CIMMERIAN IS STILL TRYING TO **REMEMBER** IT, AS HE HALF-WALKS, HALF-STAGGERS INTO A NIGHT-SHROUDED **VILLAGE.**

SOME THINGS, HOWEVER--- NEED **PRODDING.**

THE TAVERN'S PATRONS ARE A **SURLY**, WINE-SOAKED LOT--UNITED ONLY BY A **DISTASTE** FOR LAWFUL ORDER---YET IT IS NOT **THEY** WHO CATCH THE BARBARIAN'S EYE---

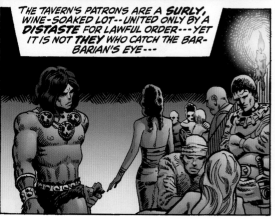

---BUT ANOTHER, MORE **ATTRACTIVE** SIGHT...!

**CONAN!**

JENNA! SO IT WAS *CORINTHIA* CALLED YOU, THE NIGHT YOU FLED *SHADIZAR* -- WITH *MY* GOLD.

WHERE *IS* IT, GIRL?

A-ALL GONE, CONAN. THE *LAST* OF IT -- WENT TO *BUY* THIS RAT-HOLE.

THAT'S *TRUE* -- I SWEAR IT BY *ISHTAR*.

HAH! YOU'D SWEAR BY THE *BAT-GOD* I KILLED FOR YOU, IF YOU THOUGHT YOU'D GAIN BY IT.

BUT DON'T WORRY -- I'M JUST GLAD TO SEE A FAMILIAR *FACE* -- AND I'VE RICHES ENOUGH NOW TO *DWARF* WHAT YOU STOLE.

OH, CONAN -- YOU ARE SO *GOOD* TO *FORGIVE* THE WRONG I DID YOU.

EVEN *MORE* GOLD, DID YOU SAY?

NOT *GOLD*, WOMAN -- BUT SOMETHING FAR MORE *PRECIOUS*. *THIS* BAG IS FILLED WITH--

--- DUST?!

BY CROM, THERE WAS *SORCERY* HERE. FIVE GEMS -- ALL TURNED TO *POWDER*.

WELL, NO MATTER -- THE *REAL* PRIZE IS IN THIS *OTHER* SACK.

CONAN, IF YOU'VE *TRULY* FORGIVEN ME, THEN MAY I *SEE*--?

JENNA--?

IT -- IT *MOVED!*

HOLD!

THERE HE IS, MAGISTRATE. *THERE* IS THE BARBARIAN WE SEEK.

*WHAT* IN THE NAME OF--?

*YOU* THERE -- *SAVAGE* -- FROM THE LOOK OF YOU, YOU ARE THE *CIMMERIAN* WE MUST EXTRADITE TO *NEMEDIA*.

THEN -- YOU ARE *UNDER ARREST*.

WELL, BARBARIAN? YOU'RE SWORDLESS-- FOUR AGAINST ONE.

GOVERNOR? WHAT GOVERNOR, DOG?

DO YOU SURRENDER -- OR DO WE SEND A CARCASS TO THE GOVERNOR?

THE GOVERNOR OF NUMALIA-- WHOSE NIECE YOU SLEW.

FOR THIS THEY HOUND ME? IT WAS A MAN-HEADED SERPENT THAT KILLED THE GIRL -- NOT I.

SO SAID ONE CALLED DEMETRIO, I'M TOLD --BUT THE NEMEDIANS STILL WANT YOUR HEAD, SO---

OH-- CONAN--!

AH-- SO YOU KNOW THE ASSASSIN'S NAME, DO YOU, WENCH?

THEN PERHAPS YOU TOO SHOULD--

HO! WHAT'S THIS YOU DROPPED?

BOOTY FROM NUMALIA, NO DOUBT--

AARRH

CONAN! THAT SACK--IT HELD A--A GREEN VIPER!

JADE WHEN I PUT IT IN-- NOW ALIVE AND VENEMOUS!

BUT, I'LL PONDER SUCH MYSTERIES LATER--IF AT ALL.

THE MAGISTRATE IS--DEAD!

SEIZE THEM!

COME, GIRL--

159

# A $50 MISUNDERSTANDING

A FEW PERSONAL NOTES ON
CONAN THE BARBARIAN BY ROY THOMAS

If not for a little matter of fifty bucks, and perhaps a certain yellowbelly attitude on my part, I might well never have written even one issue of Marvel Comics' long-running **Conan the Barbarian**, let alone more than two hundred of them.

Back in the late 1960s, as Stan Lee's associate editor and in between scripting mags like **The Avengers, The Incredible Hulk, The X-Men, Daredevil, Dr. Strange**, et al., I had to read a lot of the mail that poured into Marvel's Madison Avenue offices. Not as much as Stan did, though. Our fearless leader considered it his bounden duty to read every letter that the secretary marked as of more than passing interest, and often he'd scrawl "FYI" or some other cryptic note atop a missive and pass it on to me to handle.

And one thing that both of us noticed as the decade drew to a close was that our readers were urging us to adapt fantasy from the printed media into comics format, even though that was hardly something Marvel was noted for. They wanted Edgar Rice Burroughs (Tarzan, John Carter, etc.), Doc Savage, J.R.R. Tolkien's **Lord of the Rings**—and Robert E. Howard, especially his best-known character, Conan.

And we listened. In fact, before the 1970s would end, Marvel would produce comics about all of the above except Tolkien—and we tried for that one, but his publishing company didn't want to know from comic books.

Stan himself wasn't quite certain what readers meant when they said we should do Conan or some other "sword-and-sorcery" character, and for a while I had only a foggy notion myself of what "sword-and-sorcery" was. A couple of years earlier, when the first Lancer paperback of Robert E. Howard's work, **Conan the Adventurer**, had come out, I had picked it up as much for its Frank Frazetta cover as anything else, and had expected it to be something along the lines of John Carter of Mars. It only took reading the first few pages of the story "People of the Black Circle" therein to know I had been misled by the word "Atlantis" on the back cover, and I put the paperback on a shelf for two or three years.

Some time later I happened to read Lin Carter's paperback **Thongor and the City of Magicians**, another book with a Frazetta cover, and with a hero who combined overtones of both John Carter and (as I sensed even at the time) Conan the Cimmerian. Derivative the book may have been, but I liked it.

Then one day, Stan and I were kicking around all these requests for a Marvel "sword-and-sorcery" comic, and he made a suggestion which changed the course of my creative life. He asked me to write a memo to publisher Martin Goodman to try to convince him that we should license the rights to adapt some sword-and-sorcery hero as a comic-book character. Nobody in particular—definitely not Conan—just "a sword-and-sorcery hero."

I wrote a three-page memo which I wish I'd saved, because it evidently made quite an impression on Goodman, who mentioned it to me on several later occasions when we met (which wasn't often). I stressed in the memo that sword-and-sorcery, while generally set in a fictitious ancient world, featured several elements that made it ideal for conversion into comics. Namely, there was a brawny hero... there were beautiful women... and there were heinous villains and, even more particularly, hideous and powerful monsters.

Goodman bought my reasoning, and I was authorized to offer up to $150 per issue (a larger sum then than it is now, but still no princely ransom) for the rights to some character of our choosing. Why we didn't just make up a sword-and-sorcery hero of our own, I'm not sure to this day—that would have been more in character for Marvel—but we didn't, and I think that worked out for the best for both Marvel **and** Conan.

Except that the hero I went after, initially, was Lin Carter's Thongor of Lemuria!

It's not that Conan didn't cross my mind, of course. In addition to all those letters from readers (which surely mentioned Conan far more often than Thongor), I spent a lot of time with artist Gil Kane, who had been a Robert E. Howard devotee since at least the 1950s when Gnome Press had begun reprinting his Conan stories, and Gil was a Robert E. Howard enthusiast. In fact, Gil owned a complete set of those volumes—which I later bought from him, and still own.

But Stan and I had figured that Conan, who after all was in a number of popular paperbacks by now, would undoubtedly be out of our league financially. Maybe Lin, whose name I knew from science-fiction fanzines in the early 1960s, would be more amenable. So I made an offer to his agent. Lin himself liked comics, and the idea of Thongor being a Marvel hero, but his agent dragged his feet, probably hoping we'd up the ante. But we couldn't. When Martin Goodman said "$150," he meant "$150," not "$151." Besides, I seem to recall that Stan liked the name Thongor better than Conan or Kull anyway... it sounded more like a comic book-hero.

From time to time over a couple of months, Stan would ask how things were coming, and I had to report a lack of progress. And then one night I passed a copy of the latest Conan paperback: **Conan of Cimmeria**. I glanced at L. Sprague de Camp's introduction therein, and saw the name and even address of "the literary agent for the Robert E. Howard estate," one Glenn Lord. On a whim I sent Glenn a letter (it was too complicated at Marvel to get reimbursed for phone calls back then)—offering him the grandiloquent sum of $200 per issue for the rights for Marvel to publish a **Conan** comic book. I explained politely that I had no real leeway for negotiations, but that such a comic might give the hero a whole new audience and thus be worthwhile for the estate. Amazingly, Glenn concurred— and we were in business.

That's when it sank in what I had done. I had upped Marvel's—Martin Goodman's—offer by a full third, from $150 to $200 an issue, because of my embarrassment at the former niggardly sum. But what was I going to do if Goodman refused to go along with the increase?

Up to this time, I hadn't been at all certain I would be the writer of the **Conan** comic. I might have given it, say, to young Gerry Conway, who had already sold a science-fiction novel or two, or to someone else to write. But now I realized that I had better write at least the first issue or so myself, so that, if Goodman suddenly noticed the difference and wanted his extra $50 back, I could take that sum off my writing fee. Of course, at that time I was only getting something like maybe $15 a page, so I would've been writing several pages for free. But that was better than pounding the pavements looking for a job. I figured I'd write an issue or two—then give it to another writer and go back to concentrating on my beloved superheroes.

Thus did I back unwittingly into becoming the scripter of more than 200 issues of **Conan the Barbarian, Savage Sword of Conan**, and even **King Conan** comic books and graphic novels, two years of a Conan newspaper strip, a couple of dramatic-style record albums, several TV cartoons, as well as being, in the early 1980s, a paid consultant on the movie **Conan the Barbarian**, and co-writer of the first five drafts of its sequel, **Conan the Destroyer**.

For the comic's title I suggested **Conan the Barbarian**—a phrase never precisely used, word for word, in any of the two dozen published REH tales—because that had been the title of one of the Gnome hardcovers and had thus not been used as the name of one of the newer paperbacks with which readers were far more familiar.

Stan and I never had a moment's doubt as to who should be the new mag's artist. It would be John Buscema, with whom I had previously worked on **Sub-Mariner** and **The Avengers**. John was unfamiliar with Conan, but by then I'd made it my business to read all the Howard paperbacks and I loaned several to John. He was ecstatic. This, not superheroes, was the kind of stuff he wanted to do! When do we start?

We didn't, as it turned out. Oh, I wrote a synoposis for a story to introduce young Conan to the readers and sent it to John; but just as he was about to begin drawing it, the word came down from publisher Goodman: put a cheaper artist on **Conan**!

For some reason, Martin Goodman hadn't blanched or handed me my head on a platter when the short-form contracts were written up requiring a payment of $200 per issue rather than the $150 he had authorized. But now, uncertain how big a seller **Conan the Barbarian** would be in 1970, he wanted to hedge his bets by counting the license fee as part of what Marvel paid for the artwork. That meant that John Buscema was out, because naturally he rated the company's highest page rate and would send us over-budget. Gil Kane, who had at least a similar rate, was also disqualified.

Stan suggested a couple of lesser artists then working for Marvel, but I didn't think they'd bring the kind of individualistic style I felt **Conan** needed. So I suggested young Barry Smith, then residing in his native England. Barry had done a bit of work on **X-Men, Daredevil**, mystery stories, even **Avengers**—mostly scripted by me—while he had been working in the States some months earlier without benefit of Green Card, until the INS had caught up with him and given him 24 hours to get out of Dodge. In fact, Barry and I had done one story starring a Conan prototype we called Starr the Slayer in one of Marvel's "mystery" titles, and it hadn't gone badly.

So Buscema was out, Smith was in—and the rest, as they say, is pseudo-history.

It took us an issue or two to get our bearings, as I think even a cursory glance through this volume will show. I was still feeling my way with the writing (and wince at a few lines in **Conan #1**, at least), and I'm not sure that, if I had it to do over again, I would have asked for quite so graphic a scene of "man in space" as I had Barry draw in order to establish that this was happening in a far-distant past. As for Barry, he seems to have literally frozen up, not drawing either hero or story as well as Stan and I both knew he was capable of doing. At one point he even drew Conan planting a haymaker punch on a winged demon; that became one of several panels that, as de facto editor, I had him cut out and replace with new art. I think it was Stan who decided his splash page should be replaced with a symbolic drawing, as well. Dan Adkins' professional inking helped a bit on the interiors, as did John Verpoorten's embellishing of the cover.

And yet, everything was poised to come together, I think, for both Barry and me.

With #2 I found a concept about white man-apes in the frozen north in Robert E. Howard's pseudo-historical essay, "The Hyborian Age," and wrote a plot utilizing it. Barry drew the story more as if it were slated to appear in an Edgar Rice Burroughs comic than one featuring the creations of Howard, but there was no time to have him redraw it, and anyway it looked pretty good—far better than #1. With John Buscema's younger brother Sal inking (**him** we could afford!), we charged ahead. The story, one of only two with a 1970 cover date, was quickly nominated for a Shazam award by the professionals' own Academy of Comic Book Arts.

For issue #3 I made up a tale which used a Robert E. Howard name from a poem—Zukala—for a wizard-villain. It was a fair-to-middling story, and Barry drew it well, even if tigers weren't his strong point and though Zukala wound up looking a bit like a refugee from a Steve Ditko "Dr. Strange." I did have Barry redraw some things near the end of the story. He had a winged, flying demon suddenly become "tired"—at least that was the explanation he gave me—and fall to his death when pushed out a tower window. Possible, perhaps, but not satisfying. Also, we decided that Zukala's changeling daughter shouldn't die at the end.

As it turned out, though, "Zukala's Daughter" became **Conan #5**, not #3. Stay tuned.

For #4 I decided to do something different. From the beginning I had wanted to adapt Robert E. Howard's stories as well as make up my own, but our contract with the REH estate gave us rights only to use Conan, not any particular stories. Now I got permission from Glenn Lord in a letter to adapt the story in which the Cimmerian is chronologically youngest—"Tower of the Elephant," which had quickly become my favorite **Conan** tale of all— as an issue of Conan. Either Marvel or I—I suspect Marvel—paid a little extra for the right to adapt the story, but at this point I've totally forgotten how I swung that or how much it cost. Working with Howard's actual prose, not just my couple of pages of accompanying notes, apparently turned Barry on, and he did a wonderful job. From the time Barry drew "Tower of the Elephant," there was no looking back for either of us.

I was also aware that Howard had written other fine quasi-historical stories, many of which could easily be adapted into Conan tales. In fact, writer L. Sprague de Camp had already done precisely that with several REH stories in one of the Gnome hardcovers, and was doing more of the same in the paperbacks. I thought de Camp had a good idea there, so I suggested to Glenn that I be allowed to do the same in the comics, and he agreed—again with a pittance of filthy lucre changing hands. The story I adapted first was one called "The Grey God Passes," set in ancient Ireland—and the combination of Howard's prose and the setting must have inspired Barry, because there is some beautiful, lyrical work in what became our "The Twilight of the Grim Grey God."

At this point, I realized it worked better from a chronological point of view to make "Grim Grey God" #3, then to utilize "Tower of the Elephant," and to save "Zukala's Daughter" for #5. So that's what I did, and the publishing order of **Conan** #3 and #5 was thus reversed. And it shows, with the latter being a bit cruder than #3-4, more in line with what Barry had drawn in #2.

By about this time, sales figures on **Conan the Barbarian** #1 began to trickle in, and it appeared we had a hit on our hands. Sales were very good, albeit on a smallish print run.

In my own small way, I became as inspired as Barry, and wrote an original synopsis for #6, "Devil-wings over Shadizar." I was pleased when, months later, both it and #4 became two of the five stories nominated by ACBA as the best comic-book stories of 1971. I was even prouder when I overheard two of my fellow pro writers talking about the story being good and being an adaptation of one of Howard's stories—since every word in it is mine, except for a couple suggested by Barry. Nobody seemed to notice the "Maldiz falcon" pun I slipped into the story, though.

Issue #7 was based on a Howard Conan story, "The God in the Bowl," but that was a slight little tale, and Barry and I needed to "grow" it. This we did one night while I was visiting London for the first time. In the lobby of the hotel where my wife and I were staying, Barry and I worked out scene after scene, with Barry getting so carried away with fake sword-thrusts that a few people were looking askance at us. We changed one male villain into a female (because the original story had no women characters), expanded the fight scene and a few more things, and we produced another of my favorite issues.

Meanwhile, though, things were not going as well for **Conan** as first sales reports had indicated. It would take months to learn this—around the time we were up to #12-13 or so—but each issue of the comic from #1-7 decreased in sales from the one before it

As I should have known he would, Stan Lee saved us.

Stan cheerfully admitted that sword-and-sorcery "wasn't his thing," but he was content that it had become mine, now that I'd read the whole Conan canon and decided I wasn't going to relinquish the scripting reins to anyone but would continue to write the comic myself. He didn't read the stories, but concerned himself mostly with the covers, which were the selling-point of each issue. And he saw one thing he didn't feel good about.

"Too many animals," he told me one day around the time of #7. We'd had winged demons on the cover of issue #1, which had done well—and man-apes on #2 and a giant god on #3—but after that Barry and I got very "animal-oriented" for four issues in a row. #4 showed Conan facing the giant spider from the story—#5 depicted a woman changing into a leaping tigress—on #6 he was fighting a gigantic flying bat—and now on #7 he was battling a huge serpent (albeit one with a human, snake-haired head).

Stan wanted Conan's foes, especially on the covers, to be more humanoid.

Well, that might have happened anyway, because for #8 I had adapted a leftover REH Conan synopsis into an issue, which featured towering undead warriors guarding a treasure. Still, there's also a beastly guardian of that ruined city—which Barry had drawn exquisitely as the world's biggest Gila monster—and we might have been tempted to depict it on the cover, instead. In keeping with Stan's edict, I had Barry draw Conan confronting the tall skeletons-in-armor that he had drawn on the inside.

That made Stan happy—and, when the sales figures for #8 came in many moons later, and showed that, after a seven-issue decline, that one was the first one to go **up** in sales from the preceding month—I was ecstatic.

As a matter of fact, it was the cover and sales of issue #8, and then #9, which brought **Conan the Barbarian** back from the brink of extinction—after it was actually canceled for one day!

But that's another story....

[Roy Thomas has been a writer and often editor in the comic-book field since 1965, mostly for Marvel and DC. In a 1999 Comics Buyer's Guide poll, comics fans and professionals voted him the fifth-favorite comic-book writer of the century, and the fourth-favorite editor. He considers Conan among his favorite projects in his long career. He currently writes an occasional comic and edits Alter Ego, a monthly magazine of comics history. Since 1991 he has lived on a sizable spread in rural South Carolina with his wife Dann and a "zoo" consisting of toucans, hornbills, chinchillas, dogs, donkeys, pigs, Scottish highland cattle, guinea pigs, ducks, and capybaras—not one of which has ever appeared on a comic-book cover.]

# Also from Dark Horse

## CONAN THE BARBARIAN MINI-BUST

One of the strongest characters of heroic fiction is back with a vengeance! Sculptor Jeffery Scott, well known for his long tenure at Gentle Giant Studios, has captured the true essence of Conan. Exacting in its details and measuring in at 8 1/2 inches tall, this piece brings forward a sculptural interpretation of Conan that delivers the goods, and then some.

Limited Edition, $44.99 U.S.

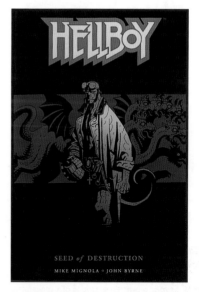

## HELLBOY: SEED OF DESTRUCTION
by Mike Mignola, John Byrne, and Mark Chiarello

When strangeness threatens to engulf the world, a strange man will come to save it. Hellboy, the world's greatest paranormal investigator, is the only thing standing between sanity and insanity as he battles the mystical forces of the netherworld and a truly bizarre plague of frogs.

$17.95 U.S., ISBN: 1-59307-094-2

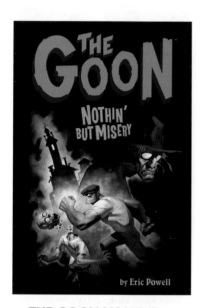

## THE GOON VOLUME 1: NOTHIN' BUT MISERY
by Eric Powell

*The Goon* is a laugh-out-loud, action-packed romp through the streets of a town infested with zombies. An insane priest is building himself an army of the undead, and there's only one person who can put them in their place: the man they call Goon.

$16.95 U.S., ISBN: 1-56971-998-5

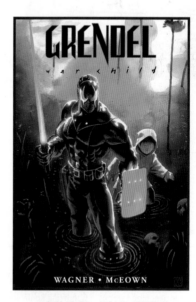

## GRENDEL: WAR CHILD
by Matt Wagner, Patrick McEown, and Bernie Mireault

Ten-year-old Jupiter Niklos Assante, heir to the throne of the Grendel-Khan, is kidnapped from the retreat in which his rapacious stepmother has hidden him, away from his rightful power. The child is worth a hefty ransom, but there seems to be more than money on the mind of his kidnapper—who is none other than the mechanical paladin, Grendel!

$18.95 U.S., ISBN: 1-878574-89-2

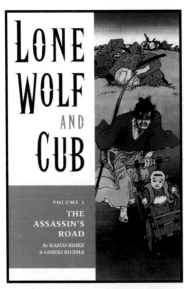

## LONE WOLF AND CUB VOLUME 1: THE ASSASSIN'S ROAD
by Kazuo Koike and Goseki Kojima,
cover by Frank Miller and Lynn Varley

Filled with unforgettable imagery of stark beauty, kinetic fury, and visceral thematic power, these stories of a vengeful samurai and his infant son have influenced a generation of visual storytellers both in Japan and in the West. *Lone Wolf and Cub* (*Kozure Okami* in Japan) is acknowledged worldwide for the brilliant writing of series creator Kazuo Koike and the groundbreaking cinematic visuals of the late Goseki Kojima.

$9.95 U.S., ISBN: 1-56971-502-5

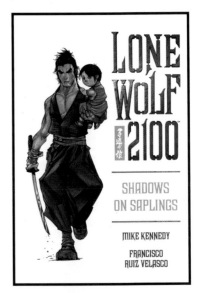

## LONE WOLF 2100 VOLUME 1: SHADOWS ON SAPLINGS
By Mike Kennedy and Francisco Ruiz Velasco

Plunge into the dystopian world one hundred years in the future, where human-like "Emulation Constructs" fight to enjoy the same rights as their human creators, where the vast majority of the world's human population struggles to eke out an existence in a hostile landscape, and where both sides are victim to corporate whim and the deadly effects of a manmade plague. An approved, ground-up re-imagining of the original *Lone Wolf and Cub* manga.

$12.95 U.S., ISBN: 1-56971-893-8

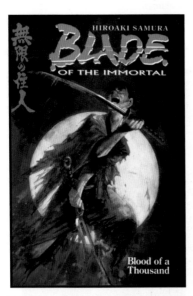

## BLADE OF THE IMMORTAL VOLUME 1: BLOOD OF A THOUSAND
by Hiroaki Samura

Kept alive by ancient blood worms, a wandering Ronin warrior called Manji is cursed with immortality and doomed to forever wander feudal Japan. To end his eternal suffering, he must slay one thousand enemies. His quest begins when a young girl seeks his help in taking revenge on her parents' killers . . . and his quest won't end until the blood of a thousand has spilled!

$14.95 U.S., ISBN: 1-56971-239-5

## THE RING OF THE NIBELUNG VOLUME 1: THE RHINEGOLD & THE VALKYRIE
by P. Craig Russell

A multiple Eisner Award winner, P. Craig Russell's adaptation of the Ring cycle by German composer Richard Wagner. The magical gold of the Rhine maidens is stolen, leading to a twisted story of vengeance and betrayal. The tainted product of the theft, a simple ring, perverts the will of everyone it comes in contact with, from the most lowly of hunchbacks to the father of the Gods.

$21.95 U.S., ISBN: 1-56971-666-8

---

**For more information on these and other books and products, visit darkhorse.com.**
To find a comics shop in your area, call the Comic Shop Locator Service toll-free at 1-888-266-4226